SERIAL CORTEX

Serial Cortex
by Chris Yee

Copyright © 2020 by Chris Yee. All rights reserved.

This is a work of fiction. Any resemblance to actual persons living or dead, businesses, events, or locales is purely coincidental. Reproduction in whole or part of this publication without express written consent is strictly prohibited.

ISBN 978-1-949218-93-0

Published by To The Moon Publishing
www.nerdchomp.com/tothemoonpublishing

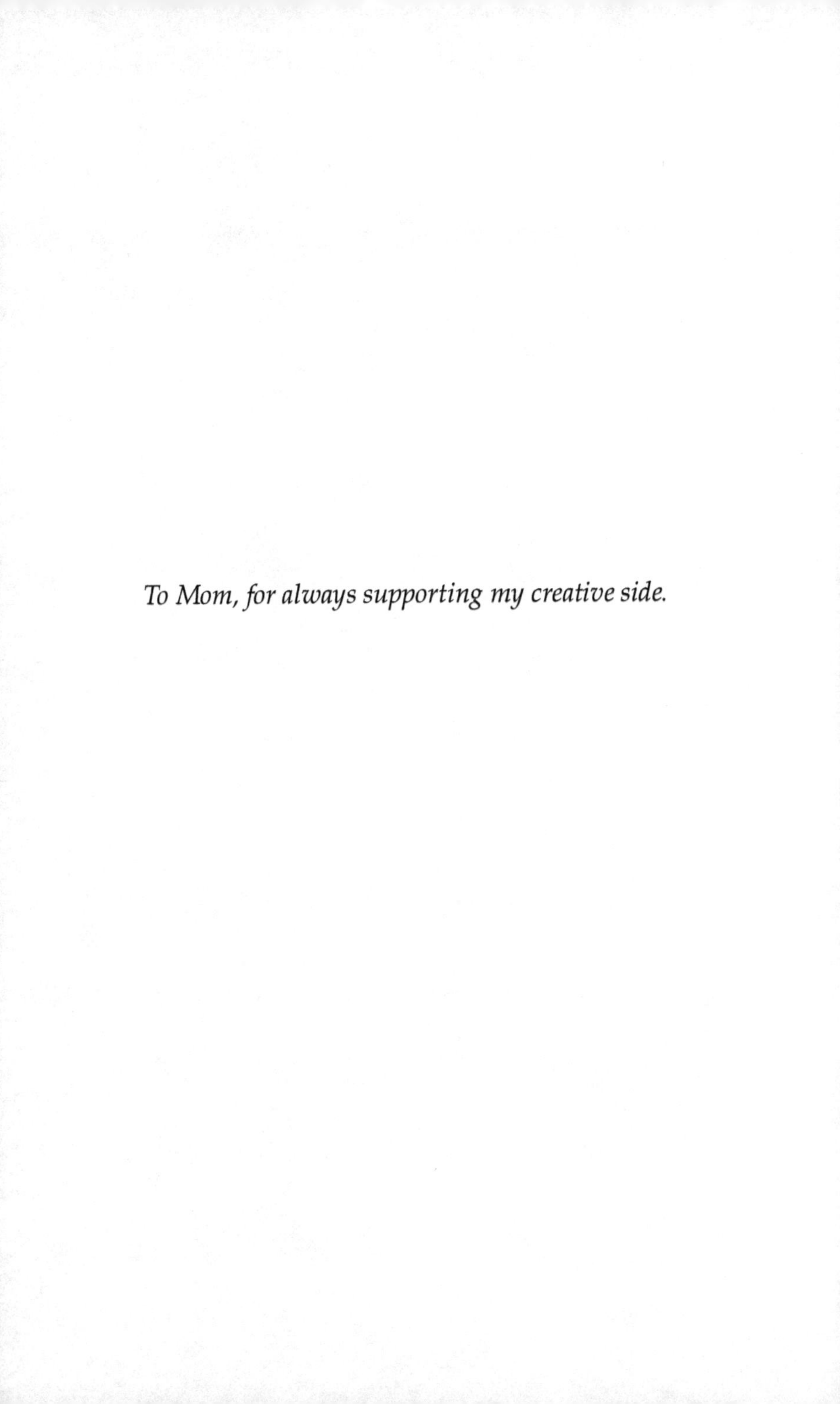

To Mom, for always supporting my creative side.

1: THE FEAR

AN ELEGANT SONG flowed from the piano as the waiters carried precarious trays of food from table to table. The intoxicating smell of fresh bread filled the air.

Hanna studied the terrified look on Dennis's face. His skin was pale and oily, hair a frizzled mess. Pockets of sweat soaked through his shirt, outlining his armpits. His chest puffed in and out as he stared at the covered dish on the table.

"Just breathe," Hanna said in the calmest voice she could manage. "You can do this. Remember why you're here. Remember why you came to me."

Dennis took a sip of wine and patted a napkin to his forehead. "I know why I'm here, but that doesn't make it any easier."

Hanna glanced at the dish. The metal cover rumbled, as if something underneath was trying to escape.

"I know it's not easy, Dennis. If it was, you wouldn't need me. But you came to me for a reason. You wanted my help. I'm here to support you. I know you can do this. You just have to trust me."

Dennis nodded. "I trust you."

"Good. Now, in a minute I'm going to ask you to remove the cover, but before you do, I want you to remember your training."

Dennis shook his head. "No. I can't do this. What the hell was I thinking?" He clenched his wine glass. "I need to get out, Hanna. Let me out."

"It's okay," Hanna said, keeping her eye on the cover. The rumbling had grown more active. "You're free to leave whenever you want, but that's not up to me. You have to remember your training. The extraction sequence, remember?"

"Right, the extraction sequence." He closed his eyes and mumbled words to himself.

Hanna reached out to grab his hand. "You're free to leave, but I urge you to stay. You wish to conquer your fear. This is the best way to do it. Face it head-on."

Dennis opened his eyes to look at Hanna.

She nodded with assurance. "You can do this."

He took a deep breath. "Okay. You're right. I can do this."

Hanna smiled. "Good. In a moment, I will ask you to remove this cover. You said you remember the extraction sequence. If at any point you feel overwhelmed, just pull yourself out. And remember, this is all in your head. You have control."

"I have control," Dennis repeated.

"That's right. Now, remove the cover."

Dennis reached out, his entire arm trembling as it moved toward the center of the table. He wrapped his fingers around the metal knob and, in one swift motion, pulled off the cover.

Sitting in the center of the plate was a black, lanky spider, no larger than a quarter. Prickly hairs covered its bulbous body and eight spindly legs extended outward. It crawled to the edge of the plate, feeling around with the tips of its legs.

Dennis froze, watching the spider climb off the plate and onto the table. His chest no longer puffed. Hanna couldn't tell if he was breathing at all.

The creature stopped at the base of their bread basket, bringing its front legs to its mouth and fiddling with its pincers. A second spider emerged from within the bread, climbing over the tops of the rolls and traversing down the side of the basket. A third spider appeared. And a fourth. They emerged from the wine glasses, and more from under the dishes.

Hanna glanced around the room. The waiters had vanished, and the piano stopped. Everyone else in the restaurant had disappeared, leaving a room full of unoccupied tables. From those tables, more spiders emerged, crawling out from under the tablecloths.

From behind the candle centerpieces. From beneath the chairs. She turned to look at the grand piano, where swarms of spiders poured out from the lid. Above, arachnids dangled from chandeliers, dropping on spindles of silk.

And back on their own table, the layer of spiders had grown so thick, Hanna could barely see the tablecloth anymore. "Dennis, you have to focus. You are in control. They're multiplying because you're letting them. You're letting this fear control your life, but it needs to be the other way around."

Tears ran down Dennis's face. "No, I want to get out. I can't do this." He closed his eyes to recite the extraction sequence.

"Please, Dennis. Don't give up. They're just spiders." She picked one up and let it crawl on her finger. "There's nothing to be afraid of."

Dennis pulled his arms away as the swarm moved toward him. More spiders climbed up his chair and onto his body.

"Breathe, Dennis," Hanna said. "Focus and remember to breathe. You're in control. Not the spiders." She locked eyes with him. "Repeat after me. I am in control."

The swarm crawled up his stomach and around his back. He tried to ignore them by focusing on Hanna. "I am in control."

"Good. Now, close your eyes and find a joyful memory. Something from your childhood. Something with a strong emotional connection."

Dennis squeezed his eyes shut, rocking in his chair.

"Do you have something?" Hanna asked.

He nodded.

"Describe it to me."

"I'm with my dad. He used to take me out for breakfast. I have a large stack of pancakes topped with strawberries, bananas, and whipped cream in front of me. My dad is eating a steak and cheese omelet."

"Good. What else? What kind of restaurant is it?"

"It's a fifties diner. The walls are covered with vintage art, and all of the employees are dressed up. There is an old jukebox in the corner."

"Is there any music playing?"

"Yes. My dad has chosen to play 'Paradise by the Dashboard Light' by Meat Loaf. I tell him it's not in the spirit of the diner, but he insists it's one of the greatest songs ever written. He's drumming on the table to the beat of the song, which is drawing the attention of the people around us. I am embarrassed, but I secretly like the song as well." A smile crept onto Dennis's face.

As he described his memory, the swarms of spiders dissipated. They retreated back into the bread baskets. Into the wine glasses. Into the piano. Back up the chandeliers. They crawled off Dennis's stomach and down the legs of his chair. They all returned to where they had come from, disappearing, and leaving only the original spider on the uncovered dish.

Dennis held out his hand and let the creature crawl on top. He raised it up to his face to watch the spider fiddle with its pincers.

The piano started to play again, and the wait staff reappeared. The surrounding tables filled up with people, bringing the ambient noise back to normal.

"Well done," Hanna said. "We've made outstanding progress today."

Relief washed over Dennis's face. He placed the spider back on the dish and smiled. "Yes, we have."

"I think that's enough for today's session. I'll see you outside."

She closed her eyes to initiate extraction.

*****

When she opened her eyes again, she was back in the lab. Dennis sat across from her in a chair that was half-reclined. His eyes were still closed. Around his head was a metal headband with a bundle of wires sticking out from the back. The wires fed up to the ceiling, suspended by brackets that guided them across the room and down into a large computer.

"How did it go in there?" a voice asked from behind.

Hanna removed her headband and turned around. Her assistant, Russell, sat in front of a large control panel, watching the glowing screens. His legs were propped on the counter and his red hair was sticking up with globs of gel. "It got a little rough," Hanna said, "but Dennis really pulled through. We had somewhat of a breakthrough today."

"That's fantastic," he said, glancing at Dennis. "It's crazy to think such a big guy could be afraid of a dinky little spider."

"Everyone has irrational fears. Arachnophobia is a pretty common one."

"I know, but look at the guy. He's buff as hell. Probably hits the gym twice a day. As a scrawny dude who has never been good at anything physical in life, it brings me great comfort knowing someone like him can be scared of something so small."

"Don't tease him, Russell. He's the only reason we're making any progress at all."

"He can't kick the crap out of me when he's unconscious. I'll tease him all I want until he wakes up."

Hanna stood up and walked over to the control panel. "Why haven't you extracted him yet?"

"He hasn't given the signal. You reminded him, right?"

"He should know the procedure. We've done it before."

Russell pointed to an image on one of the screens. "Well, he's not doing it. Must've forgot."

Hanna turned to look at Dennis. "Just pull him out anyway. No point in waiting. I'll make sure to remind him next time."

"You better," Russell said, typing commands into the keyboard. "There's a reason we have these procedures, you know."

"Just pull him out, Russell."

"Yeah, yeah. I'm getting to it." He typed one last command and hit the *enter* key. "And with the push of a button, he lives!"

Hanna rolled her eyes and walked over to help Dennis. "Welcome back," she said removing his headband. "How do you feel?"

"Amazing," Dennis answered. "I have to tell you, I was a little skeptical when we were going through the training, but this thought-hopping stuff really works."

"You did great today, but your therapy is far from over. Continued treatment is the best way to conquer your fear in the long term."

Dennis sat up, rubbing his neck. "Yes, of course. I'm just excited. I've never held a spider like that."

"It was impressive, but remember, that was only in your mind. The goal is to do it in real life. We have one ready, if you would like to try."

His excitement melted away. "I suppose I'm not quite ready for that. Maybe after a few more sessions."

"We'll give you as much time as you need. We don't want to rush you into doing anything you're uncomfortable with. Just let us know when you think you're ready."

"And next time remember to do your extraction sequence," Russell said from across the room.

Dennis peeked over Hanna's shoulder to look at Russell. "I thought I did. It didn't work?"

Hanna patted his back. "You must have done the sequence incorrectly. That's okay. We'll get it right next time. The important thing is that we've taken a step in the right direction. It should only get easier from here."

Dennis stood up to stretch his legs. "The rest of this will be smooth sailing."

"Don't get cocky," Hanna chuckled. "It will still be a lot of work, but we're certainly through the hardest part. In our next session, we'll reinforce your comfort level with that first spider. We'll try to replicate today's results to ensure a consistent response. But for now, get some rest. We'll see you tomorrow."

"Not tomorrow," Dennis said, walking to the door. "Tomorrow's my anniversary. Ten years."

"Oh, congratulations. Then the day after tomorrow. Tell Rachel I said hi."

"Will do. See you later."

Dennis left, shutting the door behind him. Hanna grabbed a small rag and wiped down the headbands.

"I still don't know why you wipe those down," Russell said. "It's not like we're sharing them. Dennis is our only client. Heck, I wouldn't even call him a client. Clients pay. Dennis is more of a moocher."

"He isn't mooching. He's helping us. We need someone to test this stuff out and no one else is willing to help. I'm grateful he's not asking us to pay him. God knows this whole thought-hopping thing is experimental. He's taking a risk on something that could easily put him in a coma."

"Let's not highlight that little detail to him."

"He knows the risks. We certainly don't hide it. But by some strange miracle he keeps coming back. Without him, our research is dead. No subjects, no testing."

"We would attract more people if we could afford nicer equipment. This lab is not very welcoming."

Hanna scanned the lab with her eyes. There were four dentist-like chairs in the center of the room, each with their own headband dangling from a hook on the back of the headrest. One of the headbands was broken, and the other three had noticeable wear.

Two of the six screens on the control panel were cracked down the center, one with a distracting flicker that distorted the image every few seconds. An old storage server sat on the counter with a wire spanning across a gap and connecting to the main computer. From within the tower of the large computer, there was an uneasy rattle.

"This place is a mess, isn't it?" she asked.

"Quite frankly, I don't know why Dennis keeps coming back."

"Don't question it. We can't afford to lose him. The best we can do is to keep this area as clean and professional as possible, and pray he sticks around. At least until we find more funding."

"I admire your optimism, but I really don't see that happening any time soon."

She pointed to one of the cracked monitors, which displayed a news anchor sitting behind a desk. "You know, I really don't like it when you watch TV while we're in there. If something happens, you need to be able to pull us out right away."

Russell shrugged. "Don't worry. I can pay attention to both."

"What were you watching, anyway?"

He stood up and grabbed a rag to help her clean the other headband. "Just the news. Apparently, they caught that serial killer."

"Serial killer?"

"Yeah, some woman killed three dudes. Stabbed them to death. Eileen Warner is her name, but the internet has dubbed her the Beantown Slasher. It's a dumb name if you ask me, but that's the internet for you."

"I didn't know there was a serial killer in the Boston area."

"That's because you're obsessed with work. Take a break. Read the news every once in a while. It's been all over the headlines. The SCB has gotten involved. They must be popping champagne over this case. After what happened in Southie a year ago, their reputation has been in the gutter. Serial Crimes Bureau? More like Serial *Slime* Bureau."

Hanna offered a perplexed look. "Slime?"

"You know, like gutter slime. Because their reputation is in the gutter."

She sustained her blank stare.

"Okay, I'll admit that wasn't my finest work, but you get my point. It looks like the SCB is finally doing something right. The Beantown Slasher is off the streets."

"As long as we're safe, that's all the matters." She waved Russell off. "Take off early. I'll close up."

"Are you sure? I don't mind sticking around."

"No, go ahead."

"Okay, but this is exactly what I'm talking about. You work too hard."

"I enjoy my work."

"That's what everyone says because they don't want to admit they've wasted an entire chunk of their life. You're one of the few people who actually means it." He grabbed his bag and slung it over his shoulder. "Don't stay too late. And don't shut off the computer. We wouldn't want to lose today's session."

"You act like I haven't done this before. I know how the system works. I built the thing."

Russell raised his hands over his head. "I'm just reminding you. Sometimes even I forget." He pushed the door open and yelled over his shoulder. "Have a good night. See you in the morning."

Hanna placed her headband down and walked to the oversized computer. An alarming warmth emanated from the case and the rattling sound had gotten worse. It was the cooling fan that needed to be replaced, but with their limited funds, every expense was significant.

Operating costs were high, and while their research was groundbreaking, they had no source of revenue. She ran her fingers over the faded Core Tech Computing logo, wondering if Russell was right. Had she wasted an entire chunk of her life? If things continued the way they were going, maybe so.

2: THE DEAL

WITH A TRAVEL mug full of fresh, hot coffee, Hanna was ready for another day. Despite Dennis's absence, there was still a checklist of tasks running through her head. First on the list was to review the footage of Dennis's prior session and record the results in a reportable format.

As she pulled into her parking spot, she noticed an unusual amount of activity. The lot was filled with unmarked black sedans, and there were well-dressed men walking in and out of the building.

She sipped her coffee and marveled at the sight of a parking lot that was usually quite empty. After a moment of observation, she stepped out of her car and walked toward the building.

When she entered the lab, Russell was near the back, talking to an older man who was dressed like all of the others. She approached them, waving to grab Russell's attention. "Russell?"

He turned around and smiled. "Here she is. Just like I said. 8 AM, right on the dot."

"What's going on? Who are all of these people?"

"Hanna, this is Charles Ward, the director of Greater Boston Homicide and the active lead for the SCB." He gestured to the man, who had long gray hair and a full beard. "Sir, this is Hanna Li."

Charles stuck out his hand. "Ms. Li, it's a pleasure to meet you. We've heard a lot of good things."

Hanna shook his hand. "It's nice to meet you as well."

Charles turned to introduce two of his acquaintances. "These are two of my brightest detectives. Meet Agents Howard Grimley and Claire Foster."

Howard was a tall man with dark brown hair and a well-defined jawline. Claire was not as tall, reaching only to Howard's shoulders. She had long blonde hair, which she had tied into a ponytail. They both wore plain black suits with SCB badges clipped to their belts.

Hanna shook both of their hands. "The Serial Crimes Bureau? I apologize for asking, but why are you here?"

Charles shook his head. "No need for apologies, Ms. Li."

"Please, call me Hanna."

"Very well, Hanna. I understand this may seem out of the ordinary. Please, allow me to explain. I assume you know about the Eileen Warner case, yes?"

Hanna tried to recall the nickname Russell had mentioned.

"The Beantown Slasher," Charles said. "Her name was all over the news yesterday."

Hanna nodded. "Yes, the Beantown Slasher. We saw you captured her."

"That's right. We have taken Eileen Warner into custody."

Russell crossed his arms, trying to achieve a professional posture. "It's great to know there's one less killer on the streets, thanks to the SCB."

"Yes, it is good news," Charles said, "but we've run into a problem. Something we believe Hanna can help us with."

"I don't understand," Hanna said. "Why would you need my help?"

Claire stepped forward. "You are the founder of Core Tech Computing, correct?"

"Yes, that's correct."

"And you specialize in cerebral infiltration?"

Hanna nodded.

Charles flashed a satisfied smile. "From what I hear, you're the leading force in this specialized field."

"It's not exactly a thriving field. It's extremely experimental, but yes, I suppose I've excelled in my research."

"She's being modest," Russell said. "She's the best there is."

"That's why we're here," Charles said. "Your expertise could be useful in the Eileen Warner case."

"I'm sorry," Hanna said. "I still don't understand. How does thought-hopping help in a serial murder case?"

"Personally, I think it's a waste of time," Howard mumbled.

Charles shot a glare of disapproval. "There's no need to be rude, Howard. We've discussed this before. You willingly stepped aside to let me lead this case. The decision is not yours to make. It's mine."

He turned back to Hanna.

"There has been a lot of discussion about whether or not we should approach you for help. Howard believes we have enough evidence to convict Eileen Warner, but I'm not so sure."

He leaned forward and lowered his own voice.

"Given the current reputation of our organization, we find ourselves backed into a corner. The public doesn't like us, and I suppose for good reason. We haven't solved a case in over a year, not to mention the disaster that happened in Southie. Innocent people died that day, and the blame was on us. This Eileen Warner case is our big break, and we can't afford to mess it up."

"I've read some of your papers," Claire said. "It's all very fascinating."

"That's right," Charles said. "Claire is the one who suggested Core Tech Computing. To be honest, I had never heard of thought-hopping before. It sounded like something out of a science fiction movie. A computer that lets you enter someone's mind."

"It's more of a visual representation of the mind," Hanna said. "The host brain sends off certain signals, and once the computer processes those signals, it stimulates similar signals in the visitor's brain. It gives the illusion of being inside someone's thoughts."

"Either way, it sounds impressive. I was skeptical at first, but the more I looked into it, the more interested I became. I guess science fiction is starting to lean more towards science than it is fiction. The way you implement the technology is clever. Helping people conquer their fears. I know a lot of people who would pay good money for that."

"It seemed like the most obvious application," Hanna said, "but there is potential for other uses as well."

"That is precisely why we are here. I believe we can use this technology for interrogation. We've already interrogated Eileen Warner through traditional methods. I can't say I expected a confession, but she's been less cooperative than I would have liked. Let me ask you a question. Can you use this technology to extract information?"

"I suppose so. Although, it's a little tougher if the host is not cooperative."

"But it is possible?"

"Yes."

"Do you think you could extract information from Eileen Warner's mind? Something to incriminate her. A memory of the murders, perhaps."

Hanna considered the question. It was certainly possible, but what were the risks? "With someone like Eileen Warner, there would be a lot of uncertainty. To extract information, she would have to be the host mind. Most of our tests have been with stable hosts. Given her background, I would assume her mind is not as reliable as we need."

She paused, running through the options in her head.

"Unfortunately, I believe it would be too dangerous. I'm flattered you've asked for my help, but I have to pass."

Charles nodded. "Very well. But before we leave, I understand you have a fairly small operation here, correct?"

Hanna nodded. "It's just Russell and I."

He glanced around the lab. "And your equipment is quite old, I see."

"Our funding has been…limited."

"What if I told you the Serial Crimes Bureau is prepared to write you a check for five-hundred thousand dollars?"

Hanna's eyes lit up. "That would be incredible. We could replace all of our equipment. Hire an assistant. Maybe even conduct some real tests."

"I figured you would like that," Charles said. He removed an envelope from his pocket. "I've always believed in emerging technology. I think it's important to invest in good ideas, and when I look at Core Tech Computing, I see a good idea. That's why I've drafted a contract. If you help us on the Eileen Warner case, the money is yours."

Hanna took the contract from his hands and scanned through the text. "It's that simple? I help you, and you pay me, no matter how successful the outcome is?"

"That's right. As long as you follow SCB policy, we are obligated to pay you five-hundred thousand dollars, regardless of the outcome. I'll let you confer with Russell, if you would like."

"No need to discuss with me," Russell said. "I'm all in. The final decision is up to her."

Hanna pointed to a line in the second paragraph. "It says here that an SCB agent will accompany me. In my professional opinion, that's a bad idea. Thought-hopping is a specialized skill. It can be dangerous for someone who doesn't know what they're doing. I wouldn't want anyone to take that risk, especially under these heightened circumstances."

"I'm afraid that part is non-negotiable," Charles said. "We need one of our agents to be there with you. Otherwise, the validity of any evidence will be brought into question."

Hanna skimmed down to the dollar amount at the bottom of the page. *$500,000*. It was enough money to steer her research in the right direction. "Okay," she said, looking up from the contract. "I will help, but only under the condition that I personally train whoever is coming along with me. I don't want any accidents."

"Neither do we," Charles said, handing her a pen. "Just sign on the bottom line."

She took the pen, scanned through the agreement one more time, and scribbled her signature at the bottom of the page.

Charles nodded and took the signed contract from her. He stuffed it back in his pocket and turned around to face Claire and Howard. "Now, which one of you wants to go through the training."

Howard raised his hand. "I'll go, sir. I know how important this case is, and I want to make sure it's done right."

Claire stepped in front of him. "Howard's done nothing but complain about bringing Core Tech Computing into this case. I'm the one who suggested them. I should be the one to go."

Charles shrugged at Howard. "She has a point."

"No offense," Howard said, "but I have more field experience than you, Claire. Given how pivotal this case is, we can't afford to make mistakes. The media is watching everything we do. One wrong step, and they'll rip us apart."

Claire propped her hands on her hips. "I'm just as competent as you, Howard. Us gals aren't as helpless as you think."

"That's not what I meant. You're putting words in my mouth. I know you're a great detective, but I have ten more years of experience under my belt. I should have seniority."

"Enough," Charles said. "If you can't make a decision, neither of you will go. I'll send Lenny instead."

"Lenny?" Howard scoffed. "He's a rookie. He doesn't know what the hell he's doing."

"Then the two of you better figure this out."

"If you don't mind," Hanna said, stepping between them. "It may not be up to you. Let me ask both of you a question. If I tell you to picture an apple, do you see an apple?"

They both stared at her with confused looks. "What do you mean?" Howard asked.

"In your mind, do you see an actual visual image of an apple. Shiny red skin. Green leaf hanging from the stem. Goofy worm with glasses popping out. You know, an apple."

Claire closed her eyes. "Yeah, I see it."

Howard scrunched his face. "You do?"

She nodded. "Yes. Are you saying you don't?"

"You're telling me you can visually see an apple?"

"Yup."

Howard shook his head. "I don't understand."

"It sounds like you have aphantasia," Hanna said.

"Aphantasia?" Howard repeated, pausing between each syllable.

"That's right. Most people have the ability to conjure an image in their mind. It's what we call, *the mind's eye.* But about three percent of the population has aphantasia. It means you don't have a *mind's eye* and you're unable to conjure a visual image in your head. Most people who have aphantasia don't realize it because no one ever talks about it. But in our case, the ability to picture something in your head is very important. It's part of our extraction method. I'm afraid if you have aphantasia, you are not suitable for thought-hopping in its current form."

"Then it's settled," Charles said. "You will train Claire, and she will accompany you during the rest of the investigation."

"How much preparation time do we have?" Hanna asked.

"Eileen Warner will arrive tomorrow afternoon, once all of the paperwork has gone through. You have until then to train Claire."

"That's not a lot of time. Ideally, training would last at least a week."

Charles shook his head. "We can't afford to wait a week. Like Howard said, the media is breathing down our neck. They're going to start questioning why we came to see you. Please understand, while your technology is impressive, it is still experimental. Spending time with something unproven will not look good in the eyes of the media. Not without results. We're risking our reputation by even coming here in the first place. It's because I believe in the technology so much that I'm willing to take that risk."

Hanna nodded. "I understand. We'll have to consolidate some of our lessons, but we can make it work."

"Good. But before you get started, we would like to conduct an interview with you to assess your initial expectations regarding the case. We'll continue to interview you throughout the process. It will help us document our progress with this new technology and evaluate its worth as a method of investigation. Agent Arthur Freeman will be in charge of these interviews. He should be around here somewhere. Claire can help you find him. In the meantime, is there a place where the rest of us can set up?"

"Yes, of course," Hanna said. "You can use the conference room. It's just down the hall. First door on the left."

"Thank you," Charles said, walking past her. "We look forward to working with you." He turned the corner, and Howard followed.

"Agent Foster," Hanna said, turning around to address her new trainee.

"Please, no need for formalities. Call me Claire."

Hanna smiled. "Okay, Claire. I'll be in my office. You can send Agent Freeman in for the interview whenever he's ready. After that, we'll get started with your training."

Claire nodded. "Very well. I'll send him your way." She exited through the front doors, leaving Hanna and Russell alone in the lab.

"Crazy morning," Russell said. "What do you think about all of this?"

Hanna took a deep breath, staring at their cracked monitors and broken headband. "Five hundred thousand dollars? I think we just caught our big break."

3: THE INTERVIEW

S ITTING IN HER office, Hanna waited in silence, listening only to the *tick* of the clock on the wall. It wasn't a sound that she usually noticed, but it was now the only thing she could focus on. Everything else was just a dream, floating by like an amorphous cloud.

The Serial Crimes Bureau. The Beantown Slasher. The five-hundred-thousand-dollar contract. None of it was real. How could it be? The biggest opportunity of her life had fallen into her lap, and now all she had to do was play along.

Her father had once told her that dreams tend to wrinkle time. That when you're dreaming, time can skip in unpredictable ways. But as she listened to the clock, it remained steady. Predictable. Time was not wrinkled, and she was certainly not dreaming. This opportunity was more than real. It was fate.

A knock at the door pulled her out of her trance. She brushed her hair back and adjusted her posture. "Come in."

A tall man entered her office wearing the same outfit as the rest of the SCB agents. He was older than the others, with greased back hair that converged into a sharp widow's peak in front. A long satchel was strapped over his shoulder, bumping against the door as he closed it. "Hello, Hanna Li," he said. His voice was low and raspy. Hanna reckoned he was a smoker. "My name is Arthur Freeman. I believe Charles has informed you I will be conducting interviews."

"Yes, he has."

"Good. That means we can get right to it." He unzipped the satchel and pulled out a tripod, setting it up in the corner of the room.

"What is that for?" Hanna asked.

Arthur reached back into the satchel to reveal a handheld camcorder. "We record a video of all interviews. I hope that's okay with you."

"Yes, of course," she said, watching him twist the camera onto the mount. "If you don't mind me asking, how long do you expect this investigation to last?"

Arthur shrugged. "I don't have a clue. That's really up to you, isn't it? You're the expert in all of this brain stuff."

"I guess that's true. It's hard for me to know for sure until I actually meet Eileen Warner. I need to learn more about her."

"You'll have plenty of time to learn about Eileen. Don't worry about that. Just don't screw this up. We have a lot riding on this case. We can't afford to have an amateur detective messing things up."

Hanna flinched at his brashness. "Excuse me?"

"I'll be frank. I think this whole thing is a waste of time. Claire and Charles are putting a lot of faith into your research, but I'm with Howard. Every minute we spend in this place is just more money down the drain. We should be doing it the old-fashioned way. You can learn a lot from just speaking to someone. How they react to your questions. Their body language. Facial tics. That's all you need. No offense, but in my opinion, thought-hopping is all theatrics and no substance. There is nothing you can learn from thought-hopping that I can't from a simple conversation."

"I respectfully disagree," Hanna said.

"Well, at least you're respectful about it. Charles just shuts my ideas down. He's always been excited about exploring new technology. I'm fine with technology. I just wish we would all slow down. Give me some time to catch up."

He flipped opened the playback screen on the camera.

"Why won't this thing turn on?" He tinkered with the buttons until the screen finally lit up. "To be honest, a part of me hopes this whole experiment fails. It'll squash this futurist vision Charles has and pull him back to reality."

"This research is very real. Cerebral infiltration is a credible field, and I believe we have a decent chance of success."

"And Charles agrees with you, which is why we're here. He has final say. He tells me to interview you, so that's what I'll do. Are you ready?"

Hanna nodded. "I am."

He pressed a button and the camera beeped, with a red light blinking above the lens. He pulled out a notepad and sat across from Hanna, jotting down notes as he spoke. "Let's get started then. Could you state your name for the camera, please?"

"My name is Hanna Li, founder of Core Tech Computing."

"Thank you, Ms. Li. Could you explain what Core Tech Computing does?"

"We specialize in a process called cerebral infiltration. Thought-hopping is the more widely used term. It's an advanced technology that allows us to interact with the world inside a person's mind. There are many potential applications for cerebral infiltration, but the one our company has chosen to focus on is fear therapy. We help our patients overcome their fears."

"Have you had success in that endeavor?"

"Yes. This field is still new, so our success is fairly limited, but we're making progress."

"Have you experimented with any other application of this technology?"

"Not a lot. In the beginning, we were mostly testing the limits of the technology. We developed a set of rules and safeguards to protect ourselves from dangerous situations."

"Yes, you've noted in some of your papers that dangerous situations can be quite common."

"They can be, if you don't know what you're doing. Like I said, we've tested our limits, and we know how to steer away from those types of things. We're still working on integrating safeguards into the software itself, but until then, we take certain precautions."

"What kind of precautions?"

"We do extensive background checks on all of our patients to make sure they're suitable for cerebral infiltration. Not everyone is. For example, one of our early subjects had a severe case of schizophrenia. We were trying to find a way to treat the condition, but the subject's mind was too fragmented. In the end, we decided the sessions were putting all of our lives in danger, so we stopped the experiment and directed them to more traditional avenues of treatment. Mental health is a large factor. We also don't accept kids. They're too impressionable."

"Are you aware of Eileen Warner's mental health?"

"I don't know the details, but from what I understand, she isn't very stable."

"No, she isn't. And knowing that, you still decided to take this job. Do you believe you can conduct this investigation under safe circumstances?"

"I do. We know the warning signs. If we encounter anything that makes us uncomfortable, we can drop out and return to the real world."

Arthur nodded, scribbling in his notepad. "I have one last question for you. Do you think thought-hopping will prove to be useful for our investigation? Will this experiment be a success?"

"It's hard to know until I learn more about the case, but I always try to stay optimistic. There are a few methods I have in mind for extracting the information we need. From what I know so far, I believe we have the tools to succeed. We just have to figure out what works with Eileen Warner. Everyone is different."

Arthur flipped his notepad shut and stuffed it into his breast pocket. "Very good. That concludes today's interview. Thank you for your time, Ms. Li."

He stood up to stop the camera.

"Charles has instructed for you to begin Claire's training as soon as you're done with me. She should be waiting in the lab. If it's okay with you, I would like to stay in your office a while longer to re-watch the video. Make sure there were no glitches. You can never trust technology to work the way it should."

"Of course," Hanna said, standing up. "Stay as long as you need."

She left her office and headed toward the lab, evaluating Arthur's questions in her head. They were all very typical questions that she had answered many times before. What was Core Tech Computing? How does the technology work?

At this point, her answers to these questions were almost automatic. Even his question about the potential dangers of thought-hopping. She had an answer ready to go. Knowing their limits in order to reduce the chance of an accident. It was a safe, diplomatic answer. Something she was sure a federal agency would want to hear. In truth, she was reluctant to reveal her doubts regarding the case.

As she entered the lab, Russell sat at the control panel and Claire watched over his shoulder. Russell noticed Hanna in the reflection of the monitors and spun his chair around. "Perfect timing. I was just booting up the training sequence. Now that you're here, we can get started with Claire."

Hanna guided Claire to the chairs in the center of the room. "Make yourself comfortable. Any of these three chairs will do. The fourth one is broken."

Claire chose the same chair that Dennis always picked, sitting and propping her legs on the extended leg rest. "Comfy."

"What a morning, huh?" Hanna asked, placing the headband on Claire.

"It's been a crazy few days," Claire said, leaning back and staring up at the ceiling. "It's a lot to take in. It must be overwhelming for you."

"To be honest, I'm flattered the SCB has so much faith in my work. Not everyone does. In fact, most people think cerebral infiltration is a waste of time."

"How can they say it's a waste of time? It's revolutionary. Your paper on phobia distortion was fascinating."

"Well, it's good to know I have at least one fan."

"I mean, using this technology to cure people's fears. It's brilliant."

Hanna chuckled. "I wish everyone was as enthusiastic about thought-hopping as you are. I think we could do great things in this field, but everyone's too scared of the tech. Nobody wants to hook up their brain to a computer. I admit, the idea is a little unsettling, and brain damage is certainly a concern…"

She stopped her train of thought and glanced over at Claire.

"Sorry. This probably isn't the best conversation to have right before your first session."

Claire waved her hand. "It's fine. I'm not worried."

"It really is safe, as long as you know what you're doing. That's why we've developed this training program."

"The sequence is ready to go," Russell said, staring at the monitors.

Hanna sat down across from Claire and put on her own headband. "Are you ready?"

Claire held up her thumb.

"Okay. Russell, put us under."

A slow drowsiness fell upon them. They both drifted out of the physical world and entered the realm of unconsciousness.

4: THE NIGHTMARE

A SWARM OF butterflies fluttered their wings, dancing around the vibrant garden. A clean brick path encircled an enclosure of bright, colorful flowers. Birds chirped cheerful melodies, chasing each other from tree to tree. The sun shined down through a haze-like mist, illuminating Hanna and Claire as they sat side by side on a small wooden bench.

Hanna turned to look at Claire, who seemed to be in a daze. "Are you okay?"

At the sound of Hanna's voice, Claire snapped out of her trance. She swiveled her head to observe their surroundings. "We're in a garden."

"That's right. This is our training simulation. It's where we start all of our newcomers."

"It's beautiful."

Hanna smiled. "Thank you. I designed it myself."

"Designed? You mean we're not in my mind right now? Or yours?"

"Correct. This is just a computer program designed to help orient first-timers like you. This simulation gives us more control over the environment than we would have if we were in someone's mind. We tried to make it as welcoming as possible."

Claire stood up and reached out to touch a flower. "Job well done."

Hanna stood up to join her. "This is where we will teach you the basics of thought-hopping. Normally, we would spend a few days in here, but given our time constraints, we'll have to consolidate a few lessons."

"I'm ready when you are."

"The first thing we'll do is record your signature."

Claire pulled her attention away from the flower to look back at Hanna. "Record my what?"

"Close your eyes," Hanna instructed.

Claire closed her eyes.

"Now, this is going to sound strange, but I am about to describe a scene to you. I want you to picture it exactly as I describe it. Try to be as visual as possible with your thoughts."

Claire acknowledged her instructions with a nod.

Hanna spoke slowly, making sure to enunciate each word with clarity. "Imagine a ship sailing in the ocean. It rocks back and forth as the waves crash against it. There is a waterfall in its path, but it does not stop. The ship continues to sail toward it, and when it reaches the waterfall, it does not fall over the edge. Instead, it floats past the edge, hovering into the air. It rises higher into the sky. Into the clouds. Sailing up above. The cloth sails transform into clouds. The wooden mast transforms into clouds. The ship's crew transforms into clouds. And soon enough, the entire ship is one giant cloud. The cloud ship maintains its form, sailing higher into the sky, rocking back and forth as the wind crashes against it."

When the words stopped, Claire opened her eyes, waiting for Hanna to continue. Waiting for more instructions.

"I got it," said an omnipresent voice, projecting from what seemed to be everywhere and nowhere all at once.

"Copy that," Hanna said, looking up at the sky. "Does it look okay or should we do it again?"

"It looks fine. No need for a redo."

Claire searched the sky for the source of the voice. "Is that Russell?"

Hanna nodded. "Yes, it is. Normally, when we thought-hop we don't have communication with him. He isn't even able to see us. It's too strenuous for the computer to process in real-time. In order to view the sessions, our computer has to render the data. It can take up to twelve hours, depending on the length of the session. But this training simulation is much less taxing on the computer. We're able to manage a live feed and full two-way communication with Russell."

"What kind of communication do we have when we're inside someone's mind?"

"None, really. That's why we took your extraction signature. While you were picturing that little scene I described for you, Russell recorded your brain activity. Your brain was performing a unique, yet very specific action, which we have saved. Everyone's brain reacts a little differently, so we've captured your own unique signature. We use this signature as a way to communicate with Russell. If you want to leave someone's mind, all you have to do is picture that ship scenario. Russell is monitoring our brain activity back in the lab. He'll see the pattern and match it with your signature. Once he confirms the match, he'll pull you out, and you'll wake up in the lab."

Claire turned back to the flower. "That's a nifty method for extraction."

"Yes, it is. It's something the two of us have developed after many years of experimentation."

"She gives me too much credit," Russell said. "It was pretty much all her idea."

Hanna waved him off. "He says that, but it's not true." She raised her voice to talk to the sky. "It's a team effort, Russell."

"I appreciate the lies," Russell said.

Hanna shook her head and grinned. "Anyway, that's extraction. Next, I want to acclimate you to the types of strangeness that can occur in someone's mind. Thoughts are weird, amorphous things. They don't always make sense in the context of the real world. Instead, they're manifestations of the host's perception of the world. If the host believes in Santa Claus, you may very well see jolly old Saint Nick just walking down the sidewalk. If the host thinks aliens exist, watch out for flying saucers."

Claire glanced up at the sky, as if she was searching for Santa's sleigh.

"But no aliens for us," Hanna said. "We start out simple. But prepare yourself. It may still be jarring."

Claire's eyes darted back and forth, readying herself for whatever was about to happen. "Back at the academy, they train us to be ready for just about anything."

Hanna smirked. "I doubt it. Go ahead, Russell. Flip the switch."

At first, nothing happened. The butterflies continued to flutter. The birds continued to sing. The sun continued to shine.

And then, it all changed at once.

The colors of the flowers shifted. Yellow to blue. White to red. Violet to orange. A wave of color pulsed through the flora and extended past the edge of the garden. The grass on the ground transformed to magenta, and then yellow, and then cyan. The leaves on the trees glowed a florescent pink as the wind rustled through their branches.

A gust of air wafted in, carrying a fresh scent of chocolate. Another gust brought cinnamon. And then cloves. The smells mixed together to form a heavenly autumn fragrance.

The sun shifted in the sky, sliding down below the horizon to reveal a starry night. The birds and butterflies transformed into glowing particles, floating toward the oversized moon. The stars pulsed in rhythm, syncing up with a choir of crickets. The brightest stars rearranged in the sky to form large pictures. A falcon. A robot. Santa Claus.

When Santa Claus formed, Hanna rolled her eyes. "Russell put that into the program. He knows I use Santa as an example, and he likes to tease me."

"It's beautiful," Claire said, watching the stars morph. "The colors. The smells. The stars. It's all stunning."

"It sure is. I've seen this sequence hundreds of times, and it never gets old."

"All of your research focuses on fear, but this right here…" Claire inhaled through her nose to capture the intoxicating aroma. "This is an experience you could sell on its own."

"We could, and I've certainly thought about it, but I believe this technology has so much more potential. I want to make an impact on the world. I want to help people. With the right amount of funding, we could really make a difference."

"You'll get your funding soon enough."

Hanna nodded. All she had to do was put a killer in jail. After that, her dreams would come true.

"Her mind won't be like this," Hanna said. "Eileen Warner's, I mean."

"What will it be like?"

Hanna shrugged. "We won't know until we go in. It depends on her personality. On her background. I don't know anything about her."

"I haven't met her in person, but her file says she has borderline personality disorder and antisocial personality disorder. Howard has talked to her. He says her behavior is sporadic. She tends to lash out at people."

"That must stem from something in her past. We'll have to dig deep to find anything useful. I anticipate her mind being worse than anything we've seen before. I hope you're prepared. We use this simulation as a pleasant way to ease people in, but our dealings with Eileen Warner will be far from pleasant."

The moving stars reached the end of their cycle and the world shifted back to the start of the transformation. Night turned to day. Flowers restored their original colors. Birds and butterflies reappeared.

"Show me," Claire said, watching a butterfly flutter in front of her.

"Show you what?"

"Show me what it will be like. You say Eileen Warner's mind will be worse than anything you've seen, so show me the worst you've seen."

"It's your first day. Do you think you can handle it?"

Claire crossed her arms. "I'm a homicide detective. Do you have any idea what kind of stuff I see on a regular basis?"

"Okay. Russell, boot up the nightmare."

"You got it," Russell said. "Just give me a second to find it."

"The nightmare, huh?" Claire asked.

"That's right. In our early days of research, we worked with a child. A boy. Only ten years old. Up until that point we had only dealt with positive emotions, but we decided to shift our focus toward fear. We figured a child's nightmare was a good place to start. So, we found Sam. His father had shown him a scary movie. A vampire flick. One of those old school Bela Lugosi vampires. You know, the scary kind."

"I love those old Dracula movies," Claire said, grinning.

"Yeah, well, this kid sure didn't. From the moment he finished the movie, he was terrified of going to sleep. He said the vampires had followed him into his dreams, and they were going to capture him and suck his blood dry."

"I'd expect nothing less from a vampire."

"I'll tell you, this movie must have had quite the impact on this kid because, when we entered his mind, it was madness."

"How bad could it be? Sure, the movie was scary back in the day, but by today's standards, it's nothing. It's really just a guy in a cape."

"You know how scary things can be when you're young. I love Ghostbusters now, but when I was a kid, those stone dog things terrified me. Everything's amplified when you're younger. Your imagination runs wild and spawns unfathomable monsters. We saw it firsthand with Sam."

The garden around them faded away, and in its place was a vast emptiness.

"One more second," Russell said. "I'm loading it up now."

"After the nightmare," Hanna continued, "we decided thought-hopping was too dangerous for kids. We sent Sam home, but we kept a recording of his session so we could learn from it. With a few tweaks in the code, Russell was able to put together a full recreation of the experience as a simulation."

The emptiness filled, and a scene formed around them. They were in a dark forest. The glowing moon peeked through a small crack in the ceiling of clouds. Lanky branches reached down from the trees like deformed arms scavenging for food, swaying as the wind tossed dead leaves onto the dirt path. The pulsing crickets were only interrupted by the occasional cautionary hoot of a lurking owl.

Claire marveled at the scene as it unfolded. "Spooky forest, huh? This is right out of Scooby-Doo."

Hanna held up her hand. "Just wait."

Another hoot echoed through the damp air. The sound was followed by the muffled screech of an owl getting snatched from its perch. A steady, guttural hiss joined the symphony of crickets. Claire glanced up at the trees, searching for the source of the skin-crawling noise.

A bush next to her rustled. Her attention darted away from the trees and toward the waist-high shrub. She squinted to peer through the darkness, leaning forward, anticipating a vampire to jump out at any moment.

Hanna observed Claire's anxious curiosity with amusement. She stepped back, cleared her throat, and pointed down the path at the monster that was soaring toward them. "Claire, look out!" she yelled in her most convincing imitation of surprise.

As Claire turned her head, the hideous creature slammed into her, knocking her to the ground. They toppled over and skidded across the dirt. Claire tumbled off the path, while the creature flipped over and landed upright. Its cape fluttered into the air and settled back down.

After a few wheezing breaths, the creature lifted its head to reveal a beast-like face. It glared at her with colorless eyes, creating the same guttural hiss from its mouth. Its skin was both pale and wrinkled, folding in unexpected ways as it moved. Two thick fangs arched out from behind its upper lip, extending longer as it flashed a menacing smile.

"Holy crap!" Claire yelled, wiping blood from her cheek. The creature's claw had slashed her face. "Is that…"

"Dracula," Hanna said, watching from the side. "And it looks like he has your scent."

The vampire arched its back like a feral cat, crawling toward her on its fingertips. It swung its head left and right, keeping its eyes locked on Claire as it moved forward. A glob of drool hung from its chin, leaving a trail of spit on the ground.

Claire jumped to her feet and backed away. "That sure as hell isn't the Dracula I know."

"No," Hanna said. "But it's the Dracula Sam knows. By the way, I would run if I were you."

Claire glanced at Hanna with growing concern. "Why?"

The creature stopped crawling and stood upright. It planted its feet into the dirt and raised its arms out to its side. From underneath its cape, two bat-like wings unfolded, blocking the moonlight and casting a long shadow onto the dirt path.

Hanna smirked. "That's why."

Dracula lunged forward, soaring through the air with incredible speed. Claire tried to run, but the vampire grabbed her and pulled her to the ground. Trapped under the monster's weight, she jammed her elbow into its face. It barely reacted to the impact at all. She tucked her knee against her chest and shoved it into the creature's stomach, again to no avail. In one final effort, she curled up, planted both feet against the vampire's waist, and pushed as hard as she could. Dracula did not budge.

It let out another guttural hiss, spraying a mist of spit into her face. Its fangs grew longer as they moved closer to her neck.

"Hanna!" Claire yelled, reaching out with her hand. "Help!"

Leaning against a nearby tree, Hanna stood with her arms crossed. She did not respond. She did not help. She only watched as Dracula plunged its fangs into Claire's neck. Claire screamed as the pointy teeth punctured her skin. Blood spurted out like juice from a tomato.

With a fresh gulp, the vampire leaned back to look at its prey, letting out a menacing laugh as he stared at her.

"Pause it," Hanna said.

The vampire froze on top of Claire with its head thrown back in laughter. The wind stopped, the crickets silenced, and the falling leaves were suspended in the air.

Claire stared at the creature's face. "He got me," she said, turning her neck to show the blood. "What does that mean? I know vampires aren't real, but it bit me."

"This is just part of the training simulation," Hanna said. "You wanted to see something dangerous. Well, here you go." She gestured to the disfigured face of Dracula. "He's programmed to ignore me and attack you, but he can't do any real damage. We have safeguards in place."

Claire crawled away from the grotesque creature, standing up and dusting herself off. "It feels so real."

"Every single experience you have is just a set of reactions in your brain. If you get hurt, your brain tells you you're hurt. When you're in here, nothing happens to your physical body, but our computer stimulates your brain in exactly the same way. Everything you feel. The wind on your skin, the cut on your face, the bite on your neck. As far as your brain is concerned, it's all real. And it will all be real when we're inside Eileen Warner's mind, with one important distinction. There will be no safeguards."

The glob of blood had trailed down Claire's neck and soaked into her shirt. She wiped it away with her palm and stared at the deep, crimson color.

"Are you still sure you want to go through with this?" Hanna asked.

Claire smeared the blood on her pants and nodded. "I know what I signed up for. I'm ready. To be honest, I'm almost looking forward to it."

"Why is that?"

"The other guys tease me. They joke that us women aren't suited for blood and murder. I know they don't mean it, but it still gets on my nerves sometimes. I feel like I have to prove myself. I have to take charge. That's why I pushed to accompany you over Howard."

"Remember," Hanna said. "You're on a live feed, right now. They can hear what you say."

A wave of panic washed over Claire.

"Nope," Russell said. "It's just me out here. Everyone else is in the conference room."

Her panic subsided. "It's nothing they haven't heard before. Sometimes I think they tease me because they know I care so much. Howard isn't as bad. He's usually the one who stands up for me."

"By the way," Russell said. "They told me the case files are ready for you, Hanna, if you want to take a look."

Hanna nodded. "Thanks, Russell. We'll wrap it up in here." She glanced back at Claire, who was examining the details on Dracula's face. "Now is the perfect time to practice sending your extraction signature to Russell. Do you remember the scene I described for you?"

Claire shrugged. "Something to do with a ship?"

"I'll repeat it for you this time, but try to remember it. It's important you're able to extract yourself without any help."

Claire nodded. "I'll pay more attention this time." She closed her eyes.

"Imagine a ship sailing in the ocean. It rocks back and forth as the waves crash against it…"

As Hanna recited the extraction sequence, Claire vanished. Russell had successfully pulled her out. Hanna closed her own eyes and pictured the cloud ship. She was ready to go back to the lab. She was eager to learn more about Eileen Warner.

5: THE CASE

HANNA AWOKE IN her chair. Claire sat across from her, shading her eyes from the bright ceiling lights. Hanna removed her headband and walked over to help her.

"Careful," she said, holding Claire's arm to prevent her from falling. "Coming back to the real world can be disorienting for first-timers."

"I'm okay," Claire said, pressing her palms into her eyes and yawning. "I'm just sleepy. This really zaps the energy out of you."

"You'll recover. It's like waking up in the morning. You're groggy at first, but you push through and get on with your day."

"Whenever you're ready," Russell said, "Charles and the others are waiting for you in the conference room."

Hanna nodded. "Thanks, Russell."

When they entered the conference room, Charles, Howard, and two other men sat at the table. One of them wore a red name tag with *Finn* written in black marker. He slouched in his chair, letting his lanky arms dangle to his sides. The man sitting next to him was taller, with glasses that were slightly too big for his face. Arthur was in the corner setting up his camera.

"Welcome, ladies," Charles said, standing up. "I hope the training is going well."

"Very well," Hanna said. "Claire is a fast learner."

"I expect nothing less of her. She's one of our best. Please, come in. I want to introduce you to a few people. You've already met Howard and Arthur."

They both waved.

"And here we have Agent Finn Dooley. He just so happened to be the crime scene investigator for all three homicides before we determined the crimes were related. It only made sense to bring him onto our team for the Eileen Warner case."

Finn stood up to shake her hand. "It's a pleasure to meet you. It's not every day I get out of the office. I'm always up for a field trip."

Charles turned to the man next to him. "And this is Agent Lenny Carver."

Lenny waved two of his fingers in what seemed to be a salute. "Morning, Ms. Li. We look forward to working with you."

"Likewise," Hanna said, sitting across from Charles.

Claire sat beside her, across from Howard.

With everyone together at the table, Finn slid three manila folders over to Hanna. "These are the case files for the three murders. Charles said you might want to take a look."

"It's important to have a good understanding of the murders," Charles said. "It might help you recognize a memory while you're in there."

Hanna opened the first folder. On top of the pile was a photo of the crime scene. It was a kitchen. Pools of deep crimson blood covered the tile floor and long red smears scaled the walls.

"That was a messy one," Charles said. "They don't get much worse than that."

"You're telling me," Finn said. "I barely held my lunch in that day. It happened in Roxbury. The victim was Anthony Higgs. He had a two-year-old daughter. We found the poor girl sitting right in the middle of that mess. God bless her soul. The victim was stabbed eighty-eight times with a kitchen knife. The high number of penetrations indicates a crime motivated by anger. To put it mildly, she was upset when she killed him."

Hanna placed the photo aside and flipped to another showing the body covered in stab wounds.

"We found Eileen Warner's hair," Charles said. "With that, we were able to place her at the scene of the crime. It's strong evidence against her, but Ms. Warner deals in prostitution, and our victim was a frequent customer. There's a chance her hair could have migrated to the victim's house through his clothes, so the hair alone is not enough to link her to the crime. We also considered the victim's girlfriend as a suspect. Stabbings like these are often a result of domestic dispute."

"But that trail led nowhere," Howard said. "His girlfriend had a solid alibi. She was working a temporary job in Maine, driving down only occasionally to visit. She punched into work that day. She wouldn't have had time to drive down."

Hanna looked up from the folder. "Maine is only a few hours drive. She could have done it."

"It's unlikely," Charles said, "but it is possible. It's one of the reasons we need more evidence."

Hanna flipped open the second folder. There was another photo of the crime scene on top, this one with far less blood.

"The second victim was Cameron Shultz in Dorchester," Finn said. "One day, he didn't show up for work, and his coworkers got worried. An officer went to check on his house and found him dead at the kitchen table. He had two daughters. One was thirteen, the other fifteen. They were both at school when it happened. Similar to the first murder, the victim was stabbed multiple times with a kitchen knife. Fifty-four times to be exact. The first one pierced his heart and killed him immediately. The rest were just for fun, I guess."

"He was eating breakfast at the time," Charles said. "He still had the fork in his hand when they found him. There were no signs of struggle. No signs he fought back. She must have snuck up on him. The back door was kicked in. That's where she must have entered."

"Was he married?" Hanna asked. "Where was his wife?"

Charles pointed to a photo of a woman. "She was our prime suspect for a while, but there wasn't enough evidence. She was working a double shift that day, and there was nothing to link her to the crime."

"That's when we found another sample of Eileen Warner's hair," Howard said. "It turns out Cameron Schultz was also one of her customers. Now, we had two connected murders, and Eileen Warner was the link. Both crimes had an excessive amount of stabbing, and the two victims were very similar. Two young fathers with loving families. Both around the same age. There was a consistent method of attack and a preferred victim profile. All the signs of a serial killer were starting to form."

"But we don't classify a serial crime unless there are at least three connected incidents," Charles said. "Two isn't enough to establish a pattern."

"Which brings us the third murder," Howard said.

Hanna grabbed the third folder and opened it. "Similar to the others, I presume."

"That's right," Finn said, leaning back in his chair. "It fit the pattern like a square peg in a square hole. It was in an apartment building in Mattapan. The tenants on the floor below had complained about a strange brown sludge seeping through their ceiling. The maintenance guy went up to investigate and discovered the body. The victim was Tucker Wright. Father of two. He had an eight-year-old son and an eleven-year-old daughter. They were at his ex-wife's house at the time of the murder. His body had sixty-one stab wounds. There were no signs of a break in, but the door was unlocked. The maintenance guy didn't need his key. He just walked right in."

Charles pointed to a photo of a young woman. "Like I said before, crimes like these are usually related to some sort of domestic dispute. Mr. Wright's girlfriend was a likely suspect, but her mother and sister both said she was with them at the time of the murder. And that's when we found..."

"Eileen Warner's hair," Hanna said, without looking up from the photo.

Howard clapped his hands together. "Bingo. I guess Ms. Warner's business was thriving. Three clients. Three murders. What are the chances of that being coincidence?"

"Pretty low," Charles said. "One murder? Sure, that kind of thing happens all the time. Two murders? It's a little strange, but not enough to raise a red flag. But three murders, all pointing back to the same woman with similar patterns and matching DNA? Now, we have a case."

"And a pretty solid one, if you ask me," Howard said.

Charles nodded. "It's a strong case against her, but from a legal standpoint, there is still reasonable doubt. Coincidence seems unlikely, but it is possible, and there's a chance a jury could see it that way too. That's why we've come to you. We need definitive proof, and Claire says you can get it for us."

"I'll try my hardest," Hanna said. "Do you have any more information about Ms. Warner herself? The more I know, the better."

"Yes, of course," Charles said. "You'll have a chance to speak with her in person when she arrives, but we can go over her profile right now. What exactly would you like to know?"

"Is there anything from her past that might be useful? Anything that would affect her emotionally, or alter her state of mind?"

"She had a poor relationship with her father. He died when she was young, but according to child services, it was probably for the best. She had bruises all over her body when they took her in."

"It falls in line with the profile of her victims," Howard said, scratching his nose. "She targets fathers."

Hanna pulled out a photo of Eileen Warner to study her face. "And her mother? What happened to her?"

"She died after giving birth," Charles said. "From what I understand, Eileen wasn't born under normal circumstances. Her mother caught an infection and died a few days after Eileen was born."

Hanna shook her head. "So, she grew up with no mother and an abusive father."

"Her upbringing has certainly affected her life," Howard said. "She's been taken into custody multiple times in the past. Mostly for prostitution and possession of drugs."

"She's also been clinically diagnosed with borderline personality disorder and antisocial personality disorder," Claire said.

"What are the symptoms?" Hanna asked.

"Self-destructive behavior. Lack of moral sense. Abandonment issues. Unstable relationships. They'll often have bouts of depression or anxiety or…" Claire paused when she noticed the worried look on Hanna's face. "What's wrong?"

"I've never dealt with such a fragile mind. You came to me because I'm an expert, but to be honest, I have no idea what we're going to find in there."

"You specialize in phobias. That must give you some experience with the unknown. That Dracula seemed pretty dangerous."

"Which is why we don't work with kids anymore. A child's mind is too unpredictable. I imagine Eileen Warner's will be worse."

"That's what science is all about," Charles said. "Pushing the limits. Learning what does and doesn't work. Exploring the unknown. There will be challenges, sure, but I believe you can overcome them. That's why we came to you, and that's why we're funding your company. Core Tech Computing is at the forefront of this technology. All you need is a little push off the deep end. After that, you can either sink to the bottom or learn how to swim." He paused, studying her face. "I think you'll swim just fine."

"And I'll be there with you," Claire said, patting her shoulder. "If you sink, we'll sink together."

Hanna raised her brow. "I don't know if that makes it better or worse."

"It makes it better, hun."

"Is there anything else you need to know?" Howard asked, standing up to stretch his legs. "If we're done, I have some paperwork to finish."

Hanna shook her head, standing up as well. "I would like to ask Eileen Warner a few more questions when she arrives, but for now, I'm all set."

"Good," Charles said. "We'll take a short lunch break and then get back to work."

They all pushed away from the table to stretch their legs. Arthur retreated to his camera, while Howard sifted through a box of files.

Charles held the conference room door open for Hanna and Claire, and walked alongside them as they made their way to the lab. "How is the training going? Will you be ready tomorrow?"

"Claire did well in the simulation," Hanna said, "but I would like to get her into a real person's mind. I'll call one of my clients to see if he can help."

"Very well. You have the rest of the afternoon. Make good use of the time."

Charles peeled off, leaving Claire and Hanna to walk alone. They entered the lab, where Russell was clacking away on his keyboard. "How did it go in there?" he asked.

"It went well," Hanna said. "Now I have a better idea of what we're dealing with. We're in for quite a ride, Russell."

"You know I'm always up for a thrill."

"Is that why you sit at the computer while I do all the dangerous work?"

"It's dangerous out here too, you know. Haven't you heard of carpal tunnel? I mean, look." He raised his hand and bent his wrist from side to side. "It's fine now, but my hand is destined to fall off eventually. That's what carpal tunnel is, right? Your hands fall off?"

"You're an idiot, Russell," Hanna said, walking past him to pick up her phone.

"Who are you calling?"

"Dennis. We need to show Claire a real person's mind."

"Dennis? Today's his anniversary, isn't it?"

Hanna shrugged. "It is, but we have no other option. We won't keep him for long."

Claire's stomach rumbled. "While you have your phone handy, let's order some food. I'm starving."

Russell's eyes lit up. "This woman has her priorities straight. Food first. Then you can call Dennis. Let's get Chinese."

6: THE BRAIN

RUSSELL SLURPED his noodles one by one, splattering grease all over his face, while Claire took a more aggressive approach, shoveling entire wads in at once. Hanna had not ordered noodles. Instead, she plucked dumplings out of her container and popped them into her mouth. A single floppy noodle whipped around Russell's lips, splashing sauce onto his shirt.

"Does he always eat this loud?" Claire asked.

Hanna chuckled. "See, Russell? I'm not the only one who thinks you eat loud."

"Hey, slurping is considered polite in Chinese culture. It shows you enjoy the food."

"I'm Chinese, and I'm telling you it's annoying."

"You're just uncultured."

Hanna turned to Claire. "It's not just with noodles. This man is the loudest chewer I've ever met."

Russell glared at her. "It's not my fault. My jaw clicks. It's a legitimate condition."

"But you refuse to have someone look at it."

"That's because I'm busy with work."

Hanna turned to Claire again. "He's just scared of the doctor."

Russell scrunched his face. "I'm not *scared* of the doctor. I just don't think it's necessary to go for every little problem you have. I have a clicky jaw, and I'm going to tolerate it like a mature adult."

"Whatever you say," Hanna said, popping another dumpling into her mouth. "Just pick up the pace. We can't sit here all day watching you eat one noodle at a time."

Russell placed his food down. "Frankly, I don't feel like eating anymore. Your negativity has killed my appetite."

"Thank the heavens," Claire said. "Now we can eat in peace."

Hanna and Claire both giggled.

"Man," Russell said. "I feel like I'm in high school again, getting teased by the popular kids. I liked it better when it was just the two of us. This Claire gal is a bad influence."

Hanna put down her empty container. "To be honest, it's kind of nice having another woman around."

Russell smiled. "Now that I think of it, this is the kind of thing I would have loved in high school. Hanging out with two girls. I'm the popular kid on the block."

The doors swung open, and Dennis entered the lab. He walked in with a wide smile on his face. "Mmm, it smells good. Chinese?"

"Sorry, Dennis," Hanna said. "None for you, unless Russell wants to share."

Russell snatched his container from the table and closed the top. "Not a chance."

"That's alright," Dennis said. "I already ate lunch."

"Thank you for coming in," Hanna said. "I know you have plans for your anniversary tonight. It means a lot that you were able to make it on such short notice. We won't keep you long, I promise."

"What is this about?" Dennis asked. "You said it was urgent." He glanced at Claire, and then back at Hanna. "Who are all of the suits?"

Claire stood up and shook his hand. "I'm Agent Claire Foster. We're with the SCB."

"The SCB? You mean serial crime stuff, right?"

"That's right. Have you seen the news recently?"

"Oh yeah. Something about the Beantown Slasher, right?"

"That's right. We believe we've captured the person responsible for those murders. That's why we've called you here."

He tilted his head. "I don't understand."

"The SCB has come for my help," Hanna said. "They want me to bring one of their agents into the suspect's mind."

Claire raised her hand. "And that agent would be me."

"But she needs more training," Hanna said. "I brought her through our simulation, but we still have time before the suspect gets here. I want to use that time to show her what a real person's mind is like."

Dennis folded his arms. "So, the two of you want to walk around my brain for a while."

"If you're willing, yes."

"Do whatever you need to do. I'm here to help as much as I can."

"Thank you. You have no idea how much I appreciate this."

He shrugged. "How can I say no to such a pretty face?"

"Again, we won't keep you long. Please, sit. Both of you." She gestured to two of the three functioning chairs.

Dennis sat in his usual seat and Claire sat beside him. They both put on their headbands and leaned back.

"Russell, are you ready?" Hanna asked as she sat in her own chair.

Russell spun around to face the control panel. "I'm ready when you are. Just say the word."

Hanna placed her headband on and nodded. "We're all set. Hit it."

*****

They were sitting in an upscale restaurant. It was the same restaurant where swarms of spiders had crawled out of nowhere. This time, there were no spiders. Claire and Hanna sat next to each other with Dennis across from them. There was a dish at the center of the table, but instead of a spider, it held an assortment of raw oysters. Dennis grabbed one and slid the slimy mollusk down his throat.

"Delicious," he said, licking his lips. "There's nothing better than a fresh oyster."

Claire twisted her head to look around the room. "Why are we here? This place is so fancy."

"This is Dennis's insular cortex," Hanna said. "The insular cortex is responsible for self-awareness. Think of it as a lobby, or a hub for us. Every time you enter a host's mind, you start in their insular cortex. Dennis is able to choose the aesthetic, and he has chosen this restaurant."

Claire turned to Dennis. "What's special about this restaurant?"

"This is where I proposed to my wife. Right at this very table." He pointed to the dish in front of them. "We had oysters that night."

Claire grinned. "That's nice."

"Yup, this place holds a special place in my heart. Just being here makes me happy."

"I was able to teach him how to change the appearance of this place," Hanna said. "That won't be the case for Eileen Warner. Her insular cortex will most likely be in her hometown. The host tends to settle on a place with strong emotional connections. Nostalgia is a big influencer. If a location isn't chosen, their hometown is a strong possibility."

Dennis nodded. "Before this restaurant, it was Vegas for me. We lived right off the strip when I was a kid. I don't have the fondest memories of Vegas, but I do get a tingle of nostalgia every time I see a photo of the house."

"Speaking of memories," Hanna said, "if Eileen Warner is guilty, she should have a memory of each murder. That's where we'll look first. We'll dig into her hippocampus, where memories are created. But first, I would like to familiarize Claire with what it's like to interact with a memory. Could we show her one of yours, Dennis?"

"Of course. What do you want to see? Any requests?"

"Anything is fine. Choose something you feel comfortable sharing with us."

He closed his eyes. "I got one." The ambient noise of the restaurant disappeared. The clanging dishes. The melodic piano. It all faded until there was only silence. The waiters froze in place, balancing trays of unserved food. The lights shut off, leaving only the glow of candles to illuminate the room.

Claire swiveled around in her chair. "What's going on?"

"Let him focus," Hanna said.

Dennis kept his eyes shut until a light across the room flickered on, illuminating a door underneath. When he opened his eyes, the lights switched back on, the waiters unfroze, and the piano picked up where it had left off. The bustling restaurant had returned to normal.

"Over there," Dennis said, pointing to the door under the light. "That's where we go."

Claire stared at the door in awe. "How did he do that?"

"Remember," Hanna said, "Dennis is the host. This is his mind. He has control. With proper training, we as visitors can control things as well, but not as effectively as the host."

"Hanna taught me well," Dennis said. "I struggled at first, but now I feel like I have more control than ever."

"You've been doing very well," Hanna said. "Your last session is proof of that."

They followed Dennis to the door, which appeared to lead to the kitchen, but when he opened it, a fresh outdoor breeze swept in. They stepped through, onto a bed of rubber mulch. Hanna bent down to pick up one of the soft nuggets, squeezing it between her fingers and flicking it away. The joyous sound of laughing children made her smile. She didn't have children of her own, but something about the bustling playground tickled her own nostalgia.

There was a large metal structure for climbing, with three red slides jutting out at different angles. On the side, there was a short climbing wall leading to the first elevated platform. Extending upward, there was a central tower where kids could look down at the adults. Separate from the main structure, there was also a jungle gym, where children could swing from end to end, or dangle from their legs to flip the world upside-down. Near the back of the playground, there was a large swing set with five standard swings and two massive tire swings.

A figure resembling Dennis stood by the swings, pushing a little boy forward every time he swung back.

"Cute kid," Claire said. "He's yours?"

Dennis nodded. "That's my son and daughter." He pointed to a girl who was attempting to move one of the tires by herself. After watching her struggle, a young woman came over to help. "And that's my wife."

"You have a beautiful family."

"Thank you. I love them very much. This is one of my fondest memories. It's just a normal day. Nothing special. But for some reason, this particular moment stuck with me."

The Dennis-like figure turned toward them and waved.

Claire flinched at the unexpected acknowledgement. "They can see us? I thought this was a memory."

"It is," Hanna said, "but it's not a perfect recreation of what happened that day. It's more of a representation of how Dennis felt. It's a manifestation of his joy. They can see us and interact with us. We can have a conversation with them, or play with their kids. Obviously, we were not there that day, but his mind creates an interactive scene that allows us to experience the memory together.

Dennis's daughter turned away from the tire and ran toward them. She waddled up to Claire and revealed a rose from behind her back, offering it as a gift.

Claire accepted the rose from her. "Thank you, sweetie. What's your name?"

The girl shined a bashful smile. "Abby."

"Hello, Abby. My name is Claire. Thank you for the gift. That was very thoughtful of you."

Abby giggled and ran off, dashing back to the tire to try moving it again.

"What a sweetheart," Claire said, fiddling with the rose.

"They're older now," Dennis said. "This memory is six years old."

"Ouch!" Claire said, looking at her finger. A thorn from the rose had punctured her skin. "That really hurt."

Hanna nodded. "It's like the training simulation. The pain is real. All three of our brains are connected. The rose is from Dennis's mind, but the signals from his brain can send pain back to yours."

"If he has control, can't he just stop those signals?"

"It doesn't work like that. That's why it's important to remember that every danger we encounter is real. Getting hurt in here could have consequences in the real world."

"What kind of consequences?"

"Anything from an itchy nose to permanent brain damage. That's why you need to remember your extraction sequence. If you ever feel your life is at risk, recite the sequence, and Russell will pull you out. If something goes wrong and you can't remember the sequence, once I'm out, I'll instruct Russell to pull you out as well. Those few seconds it takes for me to communicate with Russell could be the difference between getting out safely and falling into a coma, so please, remember the sequence."

Claire nodded. "I'll make sure to memorize it."

"I had trouble learning it too," Dennis said. "You didn't necessarily make it easy to remember."

"That's the point," Hanna said. "It's designed to be a unique signal that Russell can easily recognize. It has to be something you wouldn't normally think of, otherwise, it would be impossible to identify."

"Well, you certainly succeeded in making it unique." He watched the copy of himself walk over to his wife and kiss her on the cheek. "Would you like to see another memory?"

"No. One is enough." She turned to Claire. "So, our plan is to search Eileen Warner's memories. If we can't find a memory of the murders, I have a backup plan. We go to her dorsolateral prefrontal cortex."

"Her dorso what?" Claire asked.

"When someone decides to tell the truth, a part of their brain lights up. It's called the dorsolateral prefrontal cortex. Think of it as the truth center of the brain. If it's okay with Dennis, I would like to show you his dorsolateral prefrontal cortex." She turned to Dennis. "It's a very private part of the brain. I'll understand if you don't want to show us."

Dennis shook his head. "If it helps the case, I can bring you there."

Again, he closed his eyes. The light breeze stopped. The squeak of the swings faded. The entire memory of Dennis and his family froze in place. Claire waited for an indication of where they would go next. This time, an LED *open* sign flickered on through the front window of a store across the street.

"Over there," Claire said, pointing to the store. "That must be it."

Dennis reopened his eyes to look. "She's catching on pretty quick."

"She is," Hanna agreed.

They crossed the street and approached the store. It was a local book shop with a bright pink awning over the entrance. The sign above the door read *Pink Diamond Books*, with a drawing of a bright pink diamond wedged into the crevice of an open book.

Hanna looked through the window, past the LED sign, to see the various books on display, strategically placed to draw the attention of potential readers. There was a large pink banner on the back wall advertising a fifty-percent-off flash sale.

"I miss this place," Dennis said. "I used to come here all the time. It's a shame it doesn't exist anymore. There's nothing better than browsing the shelves and discovering a new book."

"Yes, it is a shame," Hanna said, "but it was bound to happen. You can't beat the convenience of an e-reader."

"Obviously you would say that. You're a techie. You would take a bullet for anything with an electric current running through it."

Hanna leaned closer, examining one of the book covers. It had an image of a robot riding a horse. "I can appreciate the experience of a hard copy. It has a certain charm, but you can carry hundreds of books at the same time with an e-reader."

"True, but you can't beat the texture of real paper. It's how books are meant to be read." He turned to Claire. "What do you think? We need a tie breaker."

Claire shrugged. "I don't actually read much. Don't have the time. But when I do, I suppose I prefer the sturdy heft of a hardcover."

Dennis nodded. "That's because you're a cultured woman." He glanced at the *Sorry, We're Closed* sign hanging from the door but pushed through anyway.

They followed him inside, but instead of a quirky pink-themed book store, they found themselves in a space of emptiness. An infinite landscape of white nothingness stretched in every direction. Hanna turned around for one last look at the playground, but the door had already disappeared.

Claire marveled at the clean simplicity of the place. "Where are we?"

"This is it," Hanna said. "This is his dorsolateral prefrontal cortex."

"I expected it to be more…populated." Claire turned to Dennis. "It's a little bright in here. Can you turn it down?"

Hanna shook her head. "He has very little control over what we see in here. This is where his truths live. If he had the ability to manipulate this place, his truths wouldn't really be truths."

A ghost-like manifestation of Dennis's son appeared, older than in the previous memory. He was not opaque or transparent, but instead, translucent, with cloudy blue wisps emanating from his skin. A ghost of Dennis appeared beside him, kneeling down to meet his eyes.

"I love you, Dad," the young boy said.

Dennis's ghost embraced his son, squeezing him in his arms. "I am so proud of you, son."

The two ghosts dissolved away, leaving behind a smoky blue trail that faded into the air.

"That was sweet," Claire said. "Your son will do great things. I just know it."

"Thank you," Dennis said. "That is very kind of you to say."

"That was an example of a truth," Hanna said. "The memory of his son playing in the playground must have triggered that particular truth to reveal itself. We can reveal more if we ask him questions." She turned to Dennis. "Do you mind if we try?"

Dennis shook his head. "Not at all. Ask away."

"Okay then. Prepare yourselves. This may be frightening." She cleared her throat. "Dennis, what is your greatest fear?"

Dennis shut his eyes, knowing what was about to come. Crawling up from the ground was a ghostly four-foot-tall tarantula. Its hairy legs extended toward them as it crawled along the invisible floor. Its bulbous body twitched and wiggled as it moved.

"Holy hell!" Claire yelled, stepping back.

"There's no need to be scared," Hanna said. "Unlike the rest of the brain, this spider cannot harm you. You can't even interact with it. See?" She reached out to touch the leg of the massive spider, but her hand passed through instead. "These manifestations of Dennis's truths cause no physical sensation in your brain."

Claire kept her distance. "That doesn't make the giant spider any less terrifying."

The tarantula crawled closer to Claire, opening its pincers and letting out an unsettling clicking noise. It leaned closer to study her face, and then dissolved into the air, leaving behind another wisp of blue smoke.

"This is a method we can use on Eileen Warner," Hanna said, "assuming we don't find anything in her memories."

"Why don't we just start here?" Claire asked. "Why even look at her memories at all? This seems like a more direct way to get what we want."

"Yes, it would be if she was cooperative, but I'm guessing that won't be the case. The dorsolateral prefrontal cortex is hidden in the deeper parts of her mind, which makes it harder to access. It's simple if we're working with someone who's been trained, like Dennis, but Eileen Warner will have no training. Chances are she'll be actively uncooperative. If she has secrets, she'll want to keep them from us."

"So, memories are easier to access," Claire said, predicting where Hanna's explanation would end up.

"That's right. Memories have a huge impact on the way we shape our lives. It's usually the first thing I teach when I'm training a host. Accessing these memories can help someone identify underlying problems within their life. The amygdala is another place we access a lot. It stores a number of emotions, fear being one of them. If we want to overcome a specific fear, that's where we go. Dennis has spent a lot of time dealing with his amygdala."

"Do you use this truth center place for therapeutic purposes at all?"

"Yes. The dorsolateral prefrontal cortex is where people keep their biggest secrets. Sometimes they don't even realize they're secrets until they see them for themselves. That realization can be a transformative experience. But again, it's much harder to access this part of the mind, even with training."

Claire turned to Dennis. "I don't suppose you have any deep-seated secrets of your own?"

An apparition of Hanna formed, walking in front of them and stopping just short of where the tarantula had disappeared. She stood still, peering out at the white landscape, as if she was waiting for someone. After a moment, an apparition of Dennis appeared. He approached the smoky blue figure of Hanna, standing behind her and placing his hand on her shoulder.

"What's going on here?" Claire asked.

Neither Hanna nor Dennis responded. Hanna glanced at Dennis, whose eyes were wide open and mouth ajar. When she looked back at the blue ghosts, she noticed on Dennis's ghostly left hand that his wedding band was missing.

Hanna's ghost turned around to face Dennis's ghost. He pulled her in and brought her lips to his. He moved his hand from her shoulder to her head, running his fingers through her long silky hair. She wrapped her arms around his waist and pulled him even closer. Moans of pleasure escaped their mouths as they pressed their lips together. He slid his other hand down her back and grabbed the bottom of her shirt. She lifted her arms, allowing him to pull her shirt over her head.

"Dennis!" Hanna yelled. The kissing couple disappeared as the echo of her voice sliced through them.

She could feel the blood pumping through her face, her cheeks growing hot with frustrated rage. Her fists clenched and her body tensed as she stared at the invisible ground, not knowing what to do next. She only knew that she needed to leave Dennis's brain. She closed her eyes and extracted.

*****

Hanna ripped her headband off and marched over to the control panel.

"What happened in there?" Russell asked. "Your readings shot way up."

"Pull them out," Hanna said.

Russell spun his chair away from the computer. "Are you okay? Did something happen?"

"Russell, pull them out."

"Okay, okay. Just give me a second." He spun back around, frantically typing commands into the keyboard.

Dennis woke up, lunging forward in his chair. Claire woke up beside him.

Hanna stomped over to his chair, standing in front of him with her hands on her hips. "What the hell was that?"

Dennis raised his hands in the air. "It's nothing. It doesn't mean anything."

"Careful," Russell said, scurrying over to remove Dennis's headband before he could stand up. "We don't want to break another one."

Hanna ignored Russell. "Don't lie to me. I know what something like that means in the dorsolateral prefrontal cortex. It's the truth center, Dennis."

"I swear, it was just a stupid daydream. It really means nothing."

"You're married. You have two kids. Why the hell are you thinking about something like that?"

"Sure, I'm married, but that doesn't mean I don't have fantasies."

That word made her shudder. The thought that she was his fantasy repulsed her. "Is that why you keep coming back? Do you even care about the study, or are you just here because I'm your fantasy?"

Dennis shrugged. "I mean, the progress we've made has been amazing, but I would be lying if I said I didn't find you attractive. I've always had a thing for Asians."

Hanna clenched her fists. "Get out."

"I'm surprised you care so much. You're not married. You don't have any kids. I would think a single girl like you would take it as a compliment. You're easy on the eyes."

"Get out," she repeated.

"I don't understand what I did wrong. It was just a harmless fantasy. Pull that stick out of your butt, will you?"

Hanna charged him, grabbing his shirt and pushing him back. "Get out! Get out! Get out!"

Claire and Russell jumped forward to pry the two apart. Russell pulled Hanna away and Claire stood between them.

"What are you doing?" Russell whispered into Hanna's ear. "I don't know what happened in there, but you can't attack the man. He could press charges. We can't afford a lawsuit."

Hanna took a deep breath through her nose and let it out through her mouth. "I won't attack him. But I want him out of my lab."

Russell nodded. "Claire, could you please escort Dennis out of the building?"

Claire tugged on Dennis's arm. "Come with me."

Dennis pulled his arm away. "You don't have to drag me out. I'm leaving." He pointed at Hanna. "You need to cool your jets, lady." He turned around and walked to the door. As he pushed it open, he stopped and turned his head. "Crazy bitch," he muttered. And then he was gone.

Claire rubbed Hanna's back and looked into her eyes. "Are you okay?"

"I'm fine. I just need a moment."

"Ignore guys like that. There will always be jerks out there. The best thing to do is ignore them."

"I know. What bothers me more is his reason for being here. He didn't care about the tests. This is my life's work, and he couldn't care less. He just stuck around because he thought I was *eye candy*."

"Well, you drove away our only test subject," Russell said. "Now, if this SCB deal falls through, our research is pretty much over."

Hanna considered Russell's words. He was right. Without Dennis, her research was dead in the water. The fate of Core Tech Computing was in the hands of the SCB. The company's survival now depended on the Eileen Warner case.

Howard entered the lab, pausing when he noticed the tension in the room. "What happened? Is everything okay?"

"Everything's fine," Claire said. "We just finished another training session."

"Good timing. Eileen Warner has arrived early. She's ready whenever you are."

Hanna perked up. "I want to speak with her," she said, marching past Howard.

Claire and Howard followed her out of the lab, with Russell staying behind.

"That's the idea," Howard said. "We talk to her and see what we can learn. Charles and the others are already with her."

"No," Hanna said without turning around. "I want to speak to her alone. No SCB. Just me and her."

Howard glanced at Claire as they walked. "I don't know if we can do that. Everything needs to be on record."

"If you want her to cooperate, it needs to be just me."

Again, he glanced at Claire, this time with insistence.

"We need to be there," Claire said. "It's just how things work."

Hanna stopped to look at Claire, and then at Howard. "Fine, but you don't say a single word. I ask my questions. I answer her questions. The rest of you keep your mouths shut. Got it?"

"That works for me," Howard said.

They turned the corner and entered the conference room, where Eileen Warner waited.

7: THE SUSPECT

ILEEN WARNER SAT at the table. She wore a gray shirt and sweatpants, and her wrists were shackled to the table with a pair of handcuffs. Her long brown hair covered half of her face, but she made no effort to brush it away. She furrowed her brow and jutted out her jaw, creating an almost Neanderthal appearance. Charles sat to her right, with Finn and Lenny to her left, and Arthur in the corner with his camera. Howard walked in and sat beside Charles, whispering something into his ear. Claire sat at the far end of the table, opening the case files and flipping through the photos.

Hanna could feel Eileen's glare as she walked to her seat. She sat across from her, straightening her back and clearing her throat. "Hello, Eileen. My name is Hanna." She stuck out her hand, but Eileen did not shake it. "I already know who you are, so I suppose there's no point in you introducing yourself. I would like to start off by letting you know why you're here."

"I know why I'm here," Eileen scoffed. Her teeth were stained an ugly brownish-yellow. "I'm here because the government set me up. They all want to see me rot in jail."

"The government set you up?" Hanna asked.

"That's right. They set me up so they can make money. They're going to make a fortune off me."

"I'm sorry. I don't think I understand."

"What's not to understand? They're always lying. This is just another one of their schemes. People call them conspiracy theories, but they're not theories. They're facts."

Hanna watched her crazed eyes twitch. "That's an interesting theory…"

"It's not a theory," Eileen interrupted, slamming her fist on the table. "It's fact."

"I apologize," Hanna said in a calm tone. "I don't mean to question your facts, but why would they set you up?"

Eileen leaned forward and lowered her voice. "I would tell you if these suits weren't listening. They're all in on the scheme. You can't trust any of them. Not a single one. They're always watching. Always listening. And if you say the wrong thing, they snatch you up and feed you to the wolves. All for their own benefit."

"Benefit?" Hanna asked, tilting her head. "What kind of benefit?"

Eileen crossed her arms. "Nope. I'm not talking. It's not going to happen. Not in front of these guys. Not in front of the camera."

Hanna glared at Howard with her best *I told you so* face. Howard shrugged and whispered to Charles again.

Charles nodded and stood from his seat. "Arthur, turn off the camera. Let's give these two some privacy. I hear there's a fantastic bakery across the street. We'll grab a dozen doughnuts and come back in a half hour."

Finn shot up from his chair and scrambled to the door. "All I heard was doughnuts."

Arthur popped the camera off the tripod and followed the rest of them out of the room, leaving Hanna alone with Eileen. Hanna interlocked her fingers and placed her hands on the table. "No more suits. No more SCB. It's just me and you."

Eileen whipped her head around to look behind her. "They're always listening. What, are you wearing a wire? Did they tap the room? They think they're so clever, but I know all of their tricks."

"No. The room isn't tapped. I have no wire. It's just me and you. No one else is listening."

Eileen stared at her, tilting her head up and squinting. "Okay," she said, nodding. "I'll take your word. You know, us women have to stick together. And I'm not including that government bitch out there."

Hanna glanced through the small viewing window in the door, where she could see the back of Claire's head. "That's right. I'm not with the SCB. I'm not with the government. I'm just here to talk. Woman to woman."

"Damn right." She snorted a wad of snot to the back of her throat and swallowed. "What do you want to talk about?"

"You said the SCB set you up. Why would they do that?"

"Isn't it obvious?" She threw her head back and shouted at the ceiling, "Hollywood!"

Hanna jumped in her seat, almost falling out of her chair. "I'm sorry?"

"Hollywood, honey. It's where all of the money is. Movies. Entertainment. Celebrities. Gossip. That's all people care about."

"I'm afraid I don't follow."

Eileen slammed her hands on the table and leaned forward. "Think about it, man. They want to make a movie about me. Eileen Warner, the Beantown Slasher. I already know they've been talking with some hotshot Hollywood producers. They're trying to sell the rights to my story, but there isn't even a goddamn story to sell. It's just something they made up. Hell, they probably have a whole team of writers."

"That's quite an interesting theory."

"Quit saying it's a goddamn theory."

Hanna raised an apologetic hand. "Sorry. I'll stop doing that."

"It's fact, I tell you. They'll make a movie out of anything these days. They're running out of ideas, so now the big production studios have to sign deals with the government to fabricate stories for them. The suits get a cut of the royalties and they both win. This scheme reaches higher than you know. I think the president might even be involved."

"So, they framed you to make a big Hollywood movie."

"You're goddamn right, and it'll probably be a hit. People love this kind of trash. Killer on the loose type of deals. And when I'm finally locked behind bars, they'll find someone else to frame and make a sequel. They don't care about the people. All they care about is money. That's why I don't trust a single one of them. They're all greedy pigs."

"If it's okay with you," Hanna said, "I would like to move away from the SCB. I'm not interested in them. I want to learn more about you. Where are you from? What was your childhood like?"

"You want to know about my childhood? Why is that any of your business?"

"I just want to get to know you a little better."

Eileen shrugged. "I guess chatting with you is better than having the suits come back in. So, you want to know about my childhood. I was a shitty kid, I'll admit. They always tell you how important school is, but I learned pretty fast that it's just a way for the government to keep you in line. I dropped out, and look at me now. I'm doing just fine. No high school degree. Not a single day of college. I didn't need any of that to get by."

"They tell me you're a prostitute."

Eileen chuckled. "That's at least one thing they didn't lie about." She snorted again, this time holding one nostril closed. "Yeah, I'm a prostitute, and I'm good at it. I make a good living. I'll tell you, men are stupid. They're easy to manipulate. The funny thing is some of them don't even want sex. Some just want me to take off my shirt and do a little dance. Easiest hundred I've ever made. It's pretty pathetic what guys will pay for, but as long as they're paying, I'll keep delivering. Supply and demand. I didn't need school to learn that."

"What are your clients usually like? What kind of people are they?"

"Men. I don't turn down women, but it's mostly men."

"What kind of men? Younger? Older?"

"Middle-aged dudes who are bored of their marriage. Most have kids. They always talk about their kids. It's a little weird, to be honest, but as long as they're paying, they can talk about whatever the hell they want. Their kids, their day at the office, their mother. There was this one guy that wouldn't shut up about his new puppy."

"So, it's not a very diverse group of people."

"No, it's not. Pretty much all just rich white guys looking for a fun night away from their families. Corporate types. Some guys tell their wives they're going on a business trip and book me for a week."

"It sounds like you're popular."

"I take pride in customer satisfaction. I get lots of repeat customers because I pay attention to them. I give them what they need. They like to stay in touch afterward, so I've built up some good relationships. It's all about having a good network of contacts. A lot of my clients just give me free stuff because they like me so much."

"So, you have a close relationship with your clients. What about the three murder victims? You knew them, correct?"

"Yeah, I knew them. Tony had it coming. He was a jerk. The other two were push-overs."

Hanna recalled the three victims from the case files. Anthony Higgs was the first of the three. "Okay, let's start with Tony. Why do you say he had it coming?"

"Because he was an asshole. He never called me by my name. He would just call me bitch. I didn't mind, but he was bound to piss someone off eventually."

"And then Cameron Shultz and Tucker Wright. You say they were push-overs? How so?"

"Cam was a quiet one. Whenever he came over, we would barely speak. We just got right into it. I get it. He was shy. But Tucker was an interesting one. He wasn't the brightest guy in the world, but he was definitely a talker. He would yap on and on about his wife, complaining about every single thing she did. From what he told me, she sounded like a crazy bitch. That's why I never got married. I don't want to deal with that crap. The poor sucker probably pissed her off, and she snapped. Grabbed a knife and went psycho on him."

"I read his file," Hanna said. "His wife was at her sister's house at the time of the murder."

"That's what they tell you, but how can you really know for sure?"

"Her sister and mother both vouched for her."

"Have you spoken to either of them yourself? Have you considered the possibility that those guys out there are lying to you? Or maybe her sister and mother are lying. People lie about pettier things than that. She's family. They're obviously going to protect her, even if they know she killed him."

"I suppose I can't know for sure."

Eileen nodded. "That's what I'm saying. You have to question everything they tell you because, chances are, not of word of it is true."

"Have any of your clients ever gotten violent?"

"Some are a little rougher than others, but nothing I can't handle. I mean, look at me." She gestured to her plump body. "I don't starve myself. I know how to use my own weight to my advantage."

"But none of them have tried to hurt you."

"There were a few, I guess. But like I said, I handled them."

"How did you handle them?"

"I kicked them out, for Christ's sake. I told them to get the hell out. And they always listen. I carry a gun, just in case, but I've never had to use it."

"And what about Tony? Did he ever try to hurt you?"

Eileen shifted her eyes. "You're starting to sound like those pigs out there. What's your angle?"

"I don't have an angle. It just seems like you have a pretty dangerous job. I wouldn't be surprised if you found yourself in a position where you had to defend yourself."

"Look, Tony was an asshole, but he never tried to hurt me."

"What about Cameron and Tucker?"

Eileen leaned forward and glared into Hanna's eyes. "I didn't kill them. I had no reason to. They were good paying customers. Regulars. The way I see it, whoever killed them owes me a month of rent."

Hanna held eye contact with her. "The evidence against you is strong."

"Obviously it's strong," Eileen said, leaping from her seat, but getting pulled back down by her shackles. "That's because they made it up. They're not half-assing the damn thing. It's the government. They have the resources to do whatever the hell they want. You shouldn't trust anything they say."

"Because of the movie."

"Yes, because of the movie. They don't care about the victims or the families. All they care about is money."

Hanna spread her palms on the table. "I think I have all of the information I need. Now, I'll tell you the real reason I'm here. I own a company called Core Tech Computing. You've probably never heard of it. We're small. We specialize in an emerging field called cerebral infiltration. Thought-hopping, if you will."

Eileen sneered. "Thought-hopping? That sounds like some grade-A hippie nonsense to me."

"It's actually quite sophisticated. We have a computer that allows us to enter a person's mind. We can see their memories and search their subconscious. The SCB has hired me to infiltrate yours."

"So, you are working with them," Eileen yelled, lurching forward. "You're just another lying pig."

"I assure you, I have not lied. But regardless of whether you trust me or not, you claim to be innocent. That means it is within your best interest to cooperate. I'll enter your mind and find enough evidence to clear your name. After that, you can go home and live the rest of your life."

"Why would I trust you? They're paying you. You'll just make something up to fit their story. This whole thing is a fool's trap, and I ain't no fool. There's no way in hell I'm letting you poke around my brain."

"They aren't paying me at the moment," Hanna said. "For transparency's sake, I get paid once the case is closed."

"That's even worse. It just means they still have all the leverage. They'll keep your money until you give them what they want. The whole thing's a scam, and I'm not doing it."

"I'm afraid we don't need your permission. We will enter your mind. Whether you cooperate or not will determine how long we're in there. Like I said, if you have nothing to hide, I would advise cooperating."

"Oh, you would *advise* that? Well, I would advise you to step off. I ain't trusting no one but myself."

"So, you're choosing the hard way."

Eileen sneered. "That's right, hun. I'm not making it easy for you. I'll fight. I'll struggle. I'll make this case a living nightmare." She grinned and lowered her voice to a sinister tone. "You'll wish you never met me."

Hanna stood up. "We're done here."

"You're going to hate me when this is all over," Eileen shouted, standing up with her hands still tethered to the table as Hanna walked to the door. "You hear me? I'm going to make you miserable."

Hanna ignored her and left the room. The others were no longer gathered outside. Their voices were emanating from down the hall. She followed the sounds of conversation to the kitchen, where she found the others gathered around a box of doughnuts. Russell was in the corner, chipping away at a chunk of ice and collecting the shards in a plastic cup.

"What are you doing?" Hanna asked.

Russell glanced over his shoulder. "Finn wanted an iced coffee. I got the coffee maker going, but all of the ice in the freezer fused together. I'm chipping it apart."

Lenny walked over to observe his progress. "And Russell has decided that the best tool for the job is a boxcutter. Of all the things he could have chosen, he went with a boxcutter."

Russell continued to chip away. "The boxcutter is one of the most underrated tools. Do you have any idea how many times I use this boxcutter every day? More than you would think."

"To cut cardboard," Lenny said. "Not ice. It's not meant for ice. You're just dinging up the blade."

"The blade's fine, and it's getting the job done. If I really put my weight into it, I bet I could even split this chunk in half with just one swing."

"I'll take that bet," Lenny said, reaching for his wallet. "How much are we talking? Ten? Twenty?"

Russell stopped chipping and stretched his arm. "I'll take twenty."

"No, you won't," Hanna said. "You'll ruin the counter."

"But we need to settle this argument." Russell said. "How will we know who is right?"

"Lenny is right. The boxcutter would never make it through that ice. Argument settled. Now put that back in the freezer before it melts. You have enough ice for a cup of iced coffee."

Russell opened the freezer and tossed the chunk back inside. "Who drinks iced coffee in the winter, anyway?"

Finn shrugged. "I just prefer iced over hot."

"You know it's below freezing out there, right?"

"Record lows," Howard said. "Hasn't been this cold in over a decade. The Charles River is frozen over."

"And still not a single flake of snow," Russell said, pouring coffee over the freshly chipped ice. "We're missing the only fun part of winter. Nobody just likes the cold."

Howard scrolled through his phone. "Snow's coming soon. The forecast says it'll snow in a couple of days. Same day as that chocolate festival down the street. It's supposed to be a big one."

Russell handed the cup over to Finn. "We've got record low temperatures and an incoming snowstorm. Meanwhile, this guy is sipping on iced coffee."

Finn poked a straw through the ice and took a sip. "Look, I know it's weird, but I'm standing by it. Coffee tastes better cold."

"Blasphemous," Howard said. "The ice just waters it down." He glanced at Charles. "Do you want to weigh in on this?"

Charles grabbed a plain doughnut from the box. "I enjoy a good iced coffee every once in a while, but nothing beats dipping a plain doughnut into hot coffee and letting it soak." He dipped the doughnut and took a bite. "Hanna, you're done with Eileen. Did you get what you needed?"

"I think so, but I don't expect her to cooperate going forward."

"Neither did we. She was very resistant in our own interrogations. I was hoping she would trust you a little more, considering you're not officially with the SCB."

"I lost her trust near the end of our talk, but she did tell me a few things."

"Don't keep us in suspense," Howard said. "What did you learn?"

"I learned that she dropped out of high school when she was young. Fell into prostitution as a way to support herself. Now she makes a respectable living from her work."

"We knew all of that. Tell us something that isn't already in her file."

"She has very little respect for men. She thinks they're easy to manipulate. Specifically, married men."

Howard nodded. "That fits the killers M.O. The three victims were men, and they were all either married or in a committed relationship."

"She wasn't hostile towards them." Hanna said. "She almost sounded sorry for them."

"Maybe she sees herself as a savior. Killing these men is setting them free from the trappings of marriage."

"That's possible, I suppose, but they were also her clients. She was keen on satisfying her customers. It seems like she is willing to put up with almost anything to make a quick buck."

"Did you learn anything else?" Charles asked. "Anything pertaining to your ability to infiltrate her mind?"

"She's certainly delusional and extremely paranoid. She thinks you're framing her so you can turn her story into a Hollywood movie."

Howard chuckled. "We've worked with Hollywood in the past, but never on an open case."

"Will her state of mind impede your ability to work with her?" Charles asked.

"I don't believe so. She definitely isn't stable, but we knew that going in. I didn't notice any red flags."

"Good. And what's the status of Claire's training? Is she ready? With Eileen Warner here, I would like to get started as soon as possible."

"I agree," Hanna said. "The longer we wait, the less reliable her memories will be. Claire is ready."

"Less reliable? Will they be reliable enough to hold up in court?"

Hanna shrugged. "Tentpole memories stay strong, but newer ones tend to degrade over time. If she does have memories of the murders, it'll be hard to know what condition they're in until we see them."

"Okay," Charles said, dunking the last of his doughnut into coffee and popping it into his mouth. "Hanna, Claire, and Russell. You three get set up. Howard, escort Ms. Warner to the lab."

They all dispersed.

Russell walked alongside Hanna. "What is she like? Is she nuts? I want to know what kind of trouble we've gotten ourselves into."

Hanna kept her head forward as they walked. "It will be a different experience, for sure. She's not like Dennis. She has a rough past. We'll have to be careful."

"Are you sure you still want to go through with this? We can pull out of the deal right now."

They entered the lab, where she saw the condition of their equipment. The broken headband. The cracked monitors. No money to replace them. The research she had spent a decade developing was now on the brink of death. "No. We stick to the plan. We do this, we get paid, and we save Core Tech Computing."

8: THE GIRL

HOWARD DRAGGED EILEEN through the lab and plopped her into one of the chairs. Claire sat in the seat next to her, and Hanna across from both of them. Russell grabbed Eileen's headband, but she lunged out of her seat before he could put it on. The shackles around her ankles snagged and sent her tumbling to the floor.

Howard yanked her up and slammed her back in her seat. He held her down, dodging her sporadic kicks. "Is there something we can use to restrain her?"

"You can't restrain me," Eileen said. "There's no way in hell I'm letting you inside my head. I'll die before that happens."

Howard tightened his hold on her. "Shut up!" He turned to Hanna. "She's not going to sit still. We need to restrain her."

"I've got it," Russell said, scurrying over to a milkcrate by the control panel. After rummaging through, he pulled out a small syringe. "Here we are." He bit off the plastic cover and plunged the needle into Eileen's arm. Her thrashing slowed, her eyes rolled back, and her mouth fell open with a dribble of saliva gathering at her chin.

Howard stood back, staring at the syringe. "What is in that?"

"Passiflora. It's a sedative."

"Will that affect what we see inside?" Claire asked.

Hanna shook her head. "Not Passiflora. Benzodiazepines are the more common type of sedative, but they have adverse effects on the mind. Dissociation. Amnesia. Not ideal for our purposes. We need access to her memories. Benzos can also be lethal in large doses. We decided it's best to avoid them in general. Instead, we use a special extract of passionflower. It's a natural alternative that doesn't have as many negative effects. It usually comes as a pill, but we needed a more potent version."

Russell examined the empty syringe, placing the plastic cover back on. "This stuff will keep her under for at least an hour, and it won't mess with her memories."

"It's also safer," Hanna said. "We still have to watch her dosage, but the chance of an overdose is far less likely with this passionflower extract."

"That safety part is important," Russell said, tossing the syringe in a waste bin and placing Eileen's headband on her head. "If her mind is wacky while you're in there, it puts you in danger too."

Claire leaned back in her seat. "Wacky, huh? That's an underused word. So, you're really pushing me into the deep end."

Hanna put on her own headband. "I think you're ready. Are you having doubts?"

"Not at all. I prefer to kick things off with a bang. It's the best way to learn. I'm just glad she won't be tripping on benzos."

"We learned the hard way. We worked with someone who was out on benzos, specifically Temazepam, and I'll tell you, it was gnarly."

"Is that a technical term?"

"He almost overdosed. Apparently, one vial of the stuff is way too much for one person to handle."

Russell glanced back at the milkcrate. "I think we still have some Temazepam in there. That stuff also usually comes as a pill, but we like the strong stuff here at Core Tech. We should probably just toss it, but a part of me would hate to waste a perfectly good sedative."

Hanna cringed. "That's probably the creepiest thing you've ever said, Russell."

Charles entered the lab with Arthur and Lenny. Arthur held his tripod and camera.

"Where's the best spot to set this up?" Arthur asked. "I should probably get the monitors in frame, right?"

Hanna shook her head. "There's no live feed. Everything records to our storage server, and the computer renders it overnight. You can still set it up if you'd like, but all you'll get is footage of us sitting in these chairs."

Arthur leaned the tripod against the wall and placed the camera down. "I guess there's no point then."

"So, we won't be able to see what happens until tomorrow?" Charles asked.

"Correct. It should be ready in the morning when we first get in. Remember, what happens in there isn't physically real. It's not like we can just drop in your camera and hit record. It's a virtual visualization of signals sent to the brain. The process to convert that into a usable file is substantial."

"It takes up a lot of space too," Russell said. "Storage was an oversight when we first built this computer. We had to build an external storage server as a temporary fix."

He pointed to a plastic box-shaped case on the counter, which was attached to the main computer through a series of wires.

"It has ten NAS hard drives, each with ten terabytes of storage, all hooked up to a connected server. Eventually, when we rebuild this system, we'll consider the extra storage in our design. Until then, we have this wonky setup. But it all still works. Everything saves to the storage server, and then the main computer renders the raw data into an interactive 3D space. The raw capture files are so big that we can't afford to back them up online, but the final rendered product is small enough to store on the cloud. The whole process from capture to final render should take around twelve hours. Sometimes longer depending on the length and complexity of the session. We won't be able to see what's going on in real-time, but I will have live readings of their brain activity. That information will display on these monitors."

Howard glanced at the control panel, where the screens showed diagrams of the brain, shaded with colors and labeled with numbers. "You're acting like we know what any of that means."

Russell shrugged. "I don't know what to tell you. It's the best we can do."

"Thank you," Charles said. "The footage in the morning should be good enough. Now, let's not stall any longer. Are you ready to go in?"

Hanna held her thumb out. "I'm good to go when you are, Russell."

Russell plopped the third headband on Claire and walked over to the control panel. "Here we go. Initiating in three, two, one."

Hanna shut her eyes, preparing for whatever they would encounter inside Eileen Warner's mind. What kind of twisted perils would they see?

"Go!" Russell shouted, slamming his finger down on the keyboard.

*****

Hanna and Claire stood on an empty suburban street in the middle of the night. There was a line of modest houses along both sides of the road, each an exact copy of the one beside it. Blue door. White vinyl siding. Brick chimney. Single car garage.

None of the streetlights were illuminated and pure darkness shrouded the inside of every window. The only light came from the moon, glowing brighter and larger than ever. A strong, chilled breeze pushed a heap of dead leaves from one lawn to another. At the end of the street was a dead end, where the road widened into a circle and the houses formed a loop.

"It's a cul-de-sac," Claire said. "Reminds me of where I used to live."

Hanna turned around to look in the other direction. The road stretched endlessly far, with the same identical house repeated over and over. "This is her insular cortex. She must have lived on a cul-de-sac when she was younger. These houses probably represent the one she grew up in."

Claire folded her arms, rubbing the goosebumps away. "It feels so empty."

"People's minds vary. Some are livelier than others. It does feel oddly hollow, but that probably has something to do with the sedative."

"It's eerie. I don't like it. Let's get off the street. Do you think any of these houses are unlocked?"

Hanna walked forward, following the paved path. "Maybe, but we should be careful. Doors are usually passageways to other parts of the mind. It's how the brain tends to manifest transitions and thresholds. These doors could lead anywhere. They could dump us somewhere we don't want to go."

"So, how do we control where we go? We're looking for her memories, right?"

"We are, but that's not as simple as it sounds."

"Dennis seemed to do it pretty easily."

"That's because he was the host. The host always has more control. Eileen could bring us to her memories without any issues." She gestured to the vastness of the area around them. "But who knows where she is? And even if we did find her, there's no way she would help us. She made that pretty clear when I spoke with her earlier."

"So, what do we do? What's our next step?"

"I don't have complete control, but I do have some. When you do this for a living, you learn a few tricks."

She closed her eyes and focused, conjuring some of her strongest memories. The fluttering feeling of her first kiss. The nervous excitement of moving into a college dorm. The relentless sorrow of losing her father. They were the tentpoles of her life. The moments that shaped her into the person she was today. The memories that defined her.

"Look," Claire said, pointing at one of the houses.

A light had flipped on through one of the windows, standing out like a spotlight on a dark stage. The front door had unlatched from its frame and the wind had blown it half-open.

"That's where we go," Hanna said.

Claire gazed at her in awe. "How did you do that?"

"I'm able to connect with Eileen's mind on an emotional level, but it's something that takes years of practice."

"You're certain that door will bring us to her memories?"

Hanna nodded, walking forward. "It should, but my technique is limited. I can guide us toward her memories, but I can't choose which ones we see. That's where the host has the advantage."

"So, we're stuck sifting through memories at random?"

"The strongest memories tend to surface on top. Moments with strong emotional resonance. But recent ones can get mixed in as well. The murders were fairly recent, and I imagine they would have had a big impact on her. There's a good chance we could stumble upon one of them. There's also a chance we could be at this for a while."

"Whatever it takes."

They approached the house, crossing over the pristine lawn and climbing the stairs to the open door. An echoing hiss escaped through the opening, beckoning them to enter.

Claire reached for the doorknob, but Hanna stopped her before she could pull it open. "Remember, there could be anything behind this door. We must be careful."

Claire acknowledged her words of caution and slowly opened the door.

On the other side, they found themselves standing in a cluttered living room. Crumpled paper littered most of the floor with empty pizza boxes filling the gaps.

The glow of a small tube television illuminated the room. The screen was mostly static, with short distorted flashes of what appeared to be the 1956 film, *Love Me Tender*, starring Elvis Presley. The television was muted, and the only sound in the room was the harsh *tick* of a clock on the wall.

A girl was lying on the couch, no older than ten. Her face was damp with fresh tears.

"Is that Eileen?" Claire whispered.

Hanna nodded. "Most likely. Or a memory of her, at least."

The girl, whose attention was fixed on the television, noticed the two of them standing by the entrance. She wiped her face with her sleeve and stared at them, remaining on the couch.

The kitchen light was on behind her, where a large man sat alone at a table. Gathered in front of him was a cluster of empty beer bottles. The man stared at a half-drunken beer, swaying in his seat and mumbling to himself.

"Eileen," the man called.

Panic invaded the girl's face. Her body went stiff and her eyes shut.

"Eileen," he said again, this time less enthused. He stumbled out of his seat, falling to the floor, but lifting himself back up. He walked from the kitchen to the living room, dragging his feet along the dusty carpet. "Hey, you answer when I talk to you."

He leaned over the back of the couch to look at her. The girl didn't move. She kept her eyes shut.

"Is she sleeping?" the man mumbled, glancing at Claire and Hanna.

"Yes," Claire said. "You shouldn't wake her."

He circled around to the front of the couch. "Stupid kid. That's why you don't stay up this late. You fall asleep with the TV on and waste all the goddamn power." He leaned forward to examine her face. "Are you really asleep?"

The girl remained as still as she could, but Hanna could see her arms trembling. "Yes, she is. There's no need to disturb her."

The man spun around and glared at both of them with bloodshot eyes. "I'm not asking you. I'm asking her. I don't think she is asleep. I think she can hear me just fine, and she chooses to ignore me because she's an entitled little brat. Here, I'll prove it." He undid his belt, pulling it from the waist of his pants and folding it in half.

"No," the girl whimpered, curling up on the far side of the couch. "Please, don't."

"See?" the man said, holding the belt up in his hand. "Just a little persuasion and the truth comes out. Because she knows she shouldn't be lying, right, honey?"

Tears gathered in Eileen's eyes again. "I'm sorry, sir. I didn't mean to lie."

"Did you hear that? She says she didn't mean to lie. I guess that makes you a genius now, doesn't it? Because I've lied a lot over the years, and every single time I've meant it. I'm not sure how in the world you would lie to someone without meaning it but, apparently, little miss genius has figured out a way. She's cracked the code. She's up there with Albert Einstein himself because she somehow managed to lie without meaning it. But the fact remains. You did lie, and liars need to be taught a lesson." He stepped toward her with the belt raised over his head.

"Stop!" Claire yelled. "Don't lay a finger on that girl."

Hanna glanced over at her. "Don't interfere. This is only a memory. It's not real."

The man twisted around and stared at Claire. "What did you say?"

"I said, don't touch her."

The man tightened his grip on the rough leather belt. "Yeah? And what if I do?"

"Then I'll stop you." Claire reached for her sidearm, but it wasn't there. Neither was her holster. It was then that she noticed she was wearing an entirely different outfit altogether.

The man grinned. "Forget something?"

As he turned back to Eileen, Claire lunged forward, crashing into his side and knocking him to the floor. He landed on a pile of pizza boxes, shaking his head and fluttering his eyes in a daze.

Claire hopped up and crouched beside the girl, offering a hand. "It's okay. You'll be safe with us."

Hanna watched from across the room. "We can't bring her with us. She isn't real."

Claire ignored her, looking into the girl's eyes. "It's up to you. You can stay here, or come with us."

Eileen looked down at her father, who was still on the ground, rubbing his head and groaning. She reached out and grabbed Claire's hand.

"Okay, hun. We'll keep you safe." She guided the girl over to Hanna. "Let's go."

"What are you doing?" Hanna asked.

"I'm not just going to leave her here with that guy."

"This is a memory. It's already happened. Taking her with us isn't going to change that. Whatever we do here doesn't affect anything. It only puts us in more danger."

"What danger?" Claire asked. "We're all—"

A wooden bat slammed into the side of her head. She dropped to the floor, bouncing off a wall on her way down. The man stood behind her, winding up for another swing.

Hanna charged forward, lifting the man up by the waist and throwing him onto the kitchen table. The empty beer bottles smashed under his weight, sending shards of glass through the air.

He pushed her away and hopped off the table to wind up another swing. Hanna raised her arms and caught the bat as it came down. She yanked it from his hands and jabbed his gut with the handle.

He keeled over, clenching his stomach, but recovered with an unexpected burst of strength. He lifted her up by the legs and slammed her down on the floor, sending the bat out of her hands and knocking the breath from her lungs. She squirmed on the floor, gasping for air as the man sat on top of her, straddling her stomach.

He raised his fist and smashed it into her face. A burst of stars invaded her vision. She tried to lift him off, but another fist caught her cheek, draining all of the strength from her body. Her arms fell limp to her sides, too exhausted to fight back anymore. Anticipating a third punch, she turned her head away.

Claire ran over and kneed him in the temple. He flopped over, landing beside the wooden bat.

"Come on," Claire said, helping Hanna up. "Let's get out of here." She ran to the girl and grabbed her arm. "Come with us, honey."

"We can't take her," Hanna said, wiping her face with her hand to see if she was bleeding. A vibrant red coated her fingers.

"I'm not leaving her," Claire said. She pulled on the girl's arm, leading her to the front door.

"Not that one," Hanna said. "Use the closet over there." She pointed to the door next to the kitchen. A light from the other side was peeking through the frame. "That will lead us to another memory."

They scurried to the closet as the man stood up. He lurched toward them with the bat in his hand. Claire opened the closet door, which did not lead to the inside of a closet. Instead, it led to a school cafeteria.

"Hurry, go through," Claire said.

Hanna ran through and spun around, waiting for Claire.

"You too," Claire said, looking at the girl.

Eileen stood where she was, staring straight ahead.

"What are you waiting for? Go!"

"She can't," Hanna said. "That's what I've been trying to tell you. She can't leave this memory."

"But that man is going to…" She trailed off, unable to finish her sentence.

The man was only a few steps away.

"Claire, we need to go now. You have to leave her. She's not real."

The bat swung into the door, inches from Claire's head as she stepped across the threshold.

Hanna and Claire peered through the open door at the man standing behind the girl. One hand was on her shoulder, the other gripped the bat. His menacing eyes stared back at them, and a grin formed on his face.

Eileen grabbed the side of the door and slowly pushed it shut. The hinges squealed a torturous pitch. Tears welled up in her eyes, and a trail of snot dripped from her nose. The door closed. And then they were gone.

9: THE LOCKER

CLAIRE STARED AT the closed door, unable to move or speak. Her cheek swelled where the baseball bat had struck. Hanna's face was worse, with multiple cuts and a smear of blood.

"Come on," Hanna said. "We have to keep moving."

Claire pulled her eyes from the door and turned around. "Why didn't she come?"

"I tried to tell you. It's something I should have explained earlier. That was a memory from Eileen's childhood. That girl wasn't experiencing the memory like we were. She is the memory. She can't leave. We can interact with memories, but we can't affect their outcome. Eileen's father beat her as a child. That's how that memory must end. Even if we killed her father. Cut off his head. He would just reappear unharmed and continue as if nothing happened."

"So, there's nothing we can do to save her?"

"There's no one to save. You have to understand that she's not real. What is real is that bat hitting your face."

Claire touched the bump on her cheek and flinched.

"It hurts, doesn't it? Just like the thorn and just like Dracula. The pain is real. The signals in your brain are real. If you get seriously hurt or die in here, it will affect you in the real world. So, we need to be more careful. We can't afford to get into another fight like that. Do you understand?"

Claire nodded. "I do."

"And if you ever feel like your life is at risk, remember your extraction sequence. Russell will pull you out right away."

Again, Claire nodded.

"Good. Now, where did that door bring us?"

The room was expansive, with high ceilings and large windows. The ceiling lights were flickering on and off, illuminating parts of the room and leaving others in darkness. There were round gray tables lined up in rows, each with nine seats alternating between navy blue, yellow, and white. The floor had black and white tiles arranged in a checker formation. The letters *NHS* were painted on the far wall in big bold letters.

"It looks like a school," Claire said.

Hanna examined a piece of paper that was taped to the wall. *Neverhill High School November Lunch Menu.* Below the header, there was a calendar displaying various meals for November. On the side, there was a note that read: *Pizza and chicken nuggets are available every day for $3. Milk and other beverages are available for an additional $1.*

Down lower, there was a drawing of a turkey with a note that read: *Get into the Thanksgiving season with our special turkey dinner, offered every Thursday this month. Includes white meat turkey breast, creamy mashed potatoes, cranberry sauce, and a mini apple pie.*

"Is this another memory?" Claire asked, peering out the window at the dense fog.

"I think so."

Claire spun around to explore the room. "Where is everyone? Where is Eileen? How can it be a memory if she isn't here?"

"I don't think this is a memory of a specific event in her life. It's more of a passive memory. You can recall a location without linking it to a specific incident. This is how she remembers her high school. I don't know why, but it feels...sad."

"She dropped out. I wouldn't expect her to have fond memories of this place."

"I guess not."

"It's a good spot to rest up after that fight, but I doubt we'll find anything useful here. Where do we go next?"

Hanna pointed to the other side of the cafeteria. Amidst the flickering lights, there was one continuously lit path leading out to the main hallway. "When in doubt, follow the lights."

They weaved through the rows of tables and followed the path into the hallway. The walls were lined with two layers of lockers, one stacked on top of the other. Scattered areas of blue paint were peeling off, exposing the rusted metal underneath. Halfway down the hall, there was one locker left wide open.

The clop of their shoes echoed off the bare walls, amplified by the total silence of everything else. At the center of each locker door, there was a small aluminum plaque that displayed a three-digit number. The numbers climbed as they walked forward. 478. 479. 480.

When they reached the open locker, 481, they stopped to look inside. The bottom was cluttered with binders and stacks of paper. At the top, there was a shelf with various knickknacks. Earrings, lipstick, and a small collection of miniature horse figurines. Below the shelf, there was a backpack hanging from a metal hook. The front of the bag had *E. Warner* printed in white letters. Hanna grabbed the bag and rummaged through the contents inside. She found more school supplies, but nothing that grabbed her attention.

Claire plucked a sheet of paper that was taped to the inside of the door. "Look. It's her report card. She was a decent student. Lots of B's. She even got an A in her writing class. She was doing so well. Why would she drop out?"

Hanna tossed the bag back into the locker, letting it fall to the bottom instead of hanging it on the hook. "Who knows? Maybe she just didn't like it. You can be good at something and not enjoy it."

"Most kids don't enjoy school. She was a bright student for at least part of high school. That kind of thing doesn't just disappear for no reason. Something must have happened."

"I'm sure her relationship with her father didn't help."

"Maybe that's why she did so well in school. She could either stay late and study, or go home to her father. It sounds like an easy choice to me."

Hanna shut the locker door to reveal red writing on the outside. Someone had used lipstick to vandalize her locker. *Slut* and *whore* were written in sloppy handwriting with a crude drawing of two stick figures having sex. Below the drawing, there was a cutout of a newspaper article. The headline read, *15-Year-Old Girl Survives Suicide Attempt*, with a photo of Eileen.

Claire leaned closer to read the article, shaking her head in disgust. "Bullies, man. They really get into your head. It was a problem back when I was in high school, and it's still just as bad now. Maybe even worse."

Hanna recalled her own time in high school. She had also dealt with bullies. They used to call her *nerd* and *teacher's pet*. She was always able to shake it off, but she never had to tolerate vandalism, and *nerd* was decidedly less hurtful than *slut*. Given her lack of self-confidence at that age, something like that would have devastated her.

"There will always be bullies," Hanna said. "The best we can do is to spread awareness."

"You're right. That's really all we can do. But technology is advancing so fast. It's enabling these kids to do horrible things. Soon enough, kids will be using this thought-hopping tech to bully other kids."

"I sure hope not, but it might be inevitable. I don't plan on integrating this tech with the internet, but someone is bound to do it. When that happens, cyber-bullies will be at their worst."

Claire stepped away from the locker. "I'm just glad I'm not a teenager anymore."

"You and me both. Let's keep moving. There's nothing else here." She pointed to the door at the end of the hall. A green exit sign was blinking above the door. They walked over and pushed through to whatever memory was next.

10: THE BUST

THE DOOR LED to the inside of an apartment complex. The room they were in was filthy. Garbage covered the floor and the carpet was stained with splotches of gray and brown. The air was filled with a haze of dust, and there was an unpleasant stench of rotten milk.

Eileen was lying on a couch with a cigarette wedged between two of her fingers. This time, she was not a little girl. She sucked in a lungful of smoke and blew it toward the ceiling. She did not bother using an ashtray. Instead, she let the end of the cigarette burn off and fall to the floor.

A CD player sat on the table beside her playing Elvis Presley's "Love Me Tender." His soothing voice filled the silence with a calm and comforting melody. Eileen tapped her feet to the rhythm of the accompanying guitar, mouthing the words as Elvis sang.

"I love this song," Hanna said. "It reminds me of my father."

Eileen twisted around to see the two of them standing behind her. She swung her feet off the end of the couch to face them. "Hey there. How's it going?" She coughed into her hand a few times, loosening the phlegm in her throat. "I didn't see you there."

Claire stepped forward to get a closer look at her face. "Are you…"

"I don't think so," Hanna said. "I think she's just another memory. Not the real thing."

Claire shrugged. "I guess the real Eileen wouldn't be this friendly."

Hanna glanced out the window, seeing nothing but dense fog. "She's out there somewhere."

"What are the two of you going on about?" Eileen asked, pressing the end of her cigarette into a coaster. "You know what? That's none of my business. Please, sit. Make yourselves comfortable. My door is always open for a fellow woman. We've got to stick together, you know."

Claire sat in a reclining chair. "I believe the same thing. I'm always surrounded by men at work."

"I feel you, sister. I'm a prostitute. It's my job to be around men. If there's one thing I've learned in all of my years of working, it's that you have to assert yourself, or else they just don't take you seriously."

Claire nodded. "I can oddly relate to that. Who knew prostitutes and SCB agents could have something in common?"

Hanna stood beside Claire. "This is strange."

"What's strange?" Claire asked.

"This memory. Why are we here? What's so important about this memory?"

"I have plenty of mundane memories," Claire said.

"Right, but we have no control over these memories. We should be seeing impactful memories, not mundane ones. The first two followed that pattern. Her abusive father and her attempted suicide. Those are both life changing moments. But this." She gestured to Eileen, who had slumped back into the couch. "This is just her hanging out in her apartment."

The song on the CD player ended. There was a short gap of silence, and then "Love Me Tender" started from the beginning again.

"I just love this song," Eileen said. "I could listen to it all day long."

"This is a good opportunity," Claire said to Hanna. "She seems like she might be willing to cooperate. Maybe we can ask her a few questions. Get some information about the case."

Hanna observed Eileen's friendly grin. Maybe Claire was right. She sat down on a wooden chair across from Claire. "Eileen. Do you mind if we ask you a few questions?"

Eileen shrugged. "Sure, why not? People don't usually care about the prostitute. It kind of makes me feel important. Like I'm a big Hollywood movie star, and you've come to ask about my next blockbuster hit."

Hanna recalled Eileen's rant about Hollywood conspiracies and felt an urge to avoid the topic. "What can you tell us about Anthony Higgs?"

"Tony? He's a good guy. Great customer. Has a bit of a mouth on him, but he pays, and that's what matters."

Hanna turned to Claire. "That's what she told me when I spoke with her alone. As long as they pay her, she's happy."

"That's right," Eileen said, pulling a box of cigarettes from her pocket and choosing another to smoke. "I'll put up with a lot of crap if they're willing to cough up the dough."

She reached for the lighter on the table, but Hanna grabbed it instead. "Please, let me." Hanna flipped up the cover and struck the flint wheel.

"Thanks, hun," Eileen said, leaning forward with the cigarette between her lips. She lined up the tip with the dancing flame and took a deep breath inward. The end of the cigarette glowed with red embers. She sealed her lips shut and let the smoke escape through her nostrils. "Tony whines about his wife all the time. It sounds like he can't stand to be around her. I guess that's why he comes to see me."

Elvis's song came to an end again. There was another short gap of silence before the player looped back to start the song from the beginning.

Eileen smiled. "I don't think I'll ever get sick of this song."

"What about Cameron Shultz and Tucker Wright?" Claire asked.

"Cam and Tucker are good guys. Tucker yaps just like Tony, but Cam is quieter. I think they're both married too. Or maybe one of them is divorced? I can't remember. I do know they have kids. All three of them. I've seen the pictures from their wallets."

Claire shifted forward in her seat. "How do you feel about their deaths?"

Eileen tilted her head to the side. "Deaths? What are you talking about?"

"The murders. Tucker was murdered two weeks ago. Cameron and Tony the week before that."

Eileen shook her head. "No, that's impossible. I saw Tucker three days ago. And Tony came by last weekend. They were fine."

"This is a memory," Hanna said to Claire. "For all we know, it could be a year old. In her world, the murders haven't happened yet."

"Murders aren't very common around here," Eileen said. "It might not look like it, but this is actually a pretty safe neighborhood. Very little crime, other than, you know, what I do. But I don't hurt nobody. Just have sex for money. Is that really so bad?"

"No gangs or dealers in the area?" Claire asked.

"Yeah, there are some dealers, but I don't consider that a crime. They're businessmen. They recognized a demand in the market, and they filled it. What's criminal about that?"

Instead of arguing, Claire just nodded.

"In terms of gangs, sure, they're around, but they'll leave you alone unless you piss them off. I stay out of their way, so we're all good. The worst thing that happens around here is petty theft. It happened just last week, actually. I must have left my car unlocked because someone snatched my hairbrush. No biggie. I bought a brand new one for a buck. Hell of a deal."

"So, Tony, Cameron, and Tucker are all safe and healthy?"

"As far as I know, they're as healthy as hornets." She smacked her lips together. "I don't know about you, but all of this chit chat is making me thirsty. Do you want anything while I'm up? I've got beer and tap water, but I suggest beer. You can't trust the tap water. The government dumps all sorts of chemicals into the pipes."

Hanna shook her head. "We're fine, thank you."

"Suit yourselves," Eileen said, getting up from the couch. "Holler out if you change your mind. I'm not getting up twice." She walked past them and into the kitchen.

"I don't think we're going to learn much from her," Hanna said. "She's just repeating everything she told me earlier. She doesn't even know about the murders."

Claire glanced around the room. "I don't know. She might be playing dumb. I told her I was SCB. We both know how she feels about the SCB."

Masked by Elvis's voice, they heard the muffled sound of car doors shutting outside.

"It still doesn't make sense to me," Hanna said. "Why is this memory so close to the surface? It just seems like a normal day."

Claire stood up and walked to the window, pushing aside the curtain to peek outside. Everything was shrouded in a nebulous mist. "I can't see a damn thing out there."

"I wouldn't expect you to see anything. She's not out there. It's not part of the memory."

Claire glanced at the clock. It was almost midnight. "Wait a minute. Is this the day that we…" She trailed off, staring at Hanna.

They could hear shuffling feet outside.

"What is it?' Hanna asked. "What's wrong?"

Eileen returned with a can of beer in her hand. "What are you all standing for? Sit down. Relax."

Elvis came to the end of his song, and the room fell into silence. They all stood still, waiting for the song to repeat. No speaking. Just the faint sound of the disk spinning in the player.

Finally, "Love Me Tender" played, and as it did, the door burst open. A squad of men stormed into the room, all armed with automatic rifles, equipped with helmets and armor. They charged forward and pointed their weapons at Eileen.

"Get down on the ground!" the squad leader yelled. "Do it now!"

Eileen dropped her unopened beer. The can hit the floor and sprayed a stream of fizz against the wall. She threw up her hands as high as she could. Her eyes shot wide open, shifting back and forth between all of the guns pointed at her.

"I said get down," he yelled again. "Or we will shoot!"

She obeyed his command, lowering down with her hands still raised. Once she was on her knees, the squad moved in and pushed her onto her stomach.

The squad leader took out a pair of handcuffs and locked them around her wrists. "Don't resist."

"I'm not resisting," Eileen said. Her voice was muffled against the floor. "What the hell is going on?"

He pulled her back up to her knees. "Is there anyone else in the apartment?"

"No, goddamn it. Will you tell me what's going on?"

Howard walked through the front door, followed by Lenny and Arthur. They all wore bulletproof vests, aiming their sidearms forward. When Howard saw Eileen was restrained, he holstered his weapon.

"Eileen Warner, you are under arrest for the murder of Anthony Higgs, Cameron Shultz, and Tucker Wright. You have the right to remain silent. Anything you say can and will be used against you in a court of law. You have the right to an attorney. If you cannot afford an attorney, one will be provided for you. Do you understand these rights?"

"What are you talking about?" Eileen asked. "I didn't murder anyone."

"Answer the question, Ms. Warner. Do you understand these rights?"

"Yes, I understand."

"With these rights in mind, is there anything you would like to say?"

"Not a chance."

Howard nodded. "Very well. Get her out of here."

The squad guided Eileen out of the building, led by Arthur and Lenny.

Howard paced around the apartment, studying her home. The CD player reached the end of its song and looped back again, opening with the calm strum of a guitar. Before Elvis's voice could start, Howard pressed one of the buttons. The song stopped, and "Jailhouse Rock" played.

"That's more like it," he said. "I love The King, but that song was just too damn slow." He bobbed his head from side to side and strutted out of the room, snapping his fingers to the new tempo.

Claire turned to Hanna. "If it wasn't obvious, this is the night we took her into custody."

"Yeah," Hanna said. "I picked up on that. Were you there that night?"

"No. I was out sick. Had a nasty fever."

Hanna walked up to the CD player to turn it off. "It's weird. It's the night you took her in, but she didn't seem to know about the murders at all."

"It could be an act. I wouldn't expect her to confess."

Hanna stared at the can of beer on the floor, which had stopped spraying and was now soaking into the carpet. "I guess not. But still, it was odd."

A spotlight from nowhere illuminated the front door.

"I assume that's where we go next?" Claire asked. "That will lead us to the next memory?"

"Correct. But I'm starting to wonder if there's a better way. We're not getting any closer to finding what we need."

"What other option do we have?"

Hanna watched the spotlight flicker. "We could try her dorsolateral prefrontal cortex. There will be definitive proof there."

"Her truth center? Do you know how to get us there?"

"Maybe. I've never done it before, but in theory, it should be similar to accessing her memories. It doesn't hurt to try. We can't just roam through memories all day without any control over them."

"Okay," Claire said, stepping aside. "Give it a shot."

Hanna stared at the spotlight. The flickering became more uniform.

On. Off. On. Off.

Like someone flipping a switch in a deliberate pattern. The rate of the flicker increased, growing more rapid with every cycle.

On. Off. On. Off.

Other lights in the room flashed, some matching the pace of the spotlight, others falling out of phase. They all grew with intensity, transitioning into a strobe light effect.

On. Off. On. Off.

The entire room fell into a dizzying swirl of disorientation with bursts of light invading from all sides. It was overstimulating. Overpowering.

And then all of the bulbs blew out, filling the room with darkness. The spotlight on the door returned, but now it was red, painting the entire room red with it.

Claire glanced around the apartment, soaking in the new sinister atmosphere. "Does that mean it worked?"

Hanna approached the door, reaching out to touch the wooden surface. "I don't know. It's the first time I've tried to access the dorsolateral prefrontal cortex without the host. I don't know how the mind reacts."

"I guess there's only one way to find out," Claire said. She walked into the red spotlight and pulled open the door.

Hanna followed with caution. The color change raised her curiosity. Was red good or bad? Or did it even matter at all? The fact that she did not know the answer bothered her.

11: THE DARK

THEY ENTERED A dark hallway. There was an unpleasant musk floating in the air. The sound of dripping water echoed off the concrete walls. A dark, shadowy aura engulfed the path in front of them. At the far end of the hall, peeking through the black fog, was another red spotlight illuminating another door.

Claire touched her hand to the wall. "It's cold. This whole place is freezing."

Hanna pointed past the floating black cloud. "It looks like there's only one way to go. We follow the red light."

She stepped into the darkness, letting the shadow consume her. A gust of wind hit her face, blowing her hair, and sending shivers through her body.

"Are you okay?" she asked Claire, without looking back.

"Yeah, I'm fine. But let's get out of this hallway. It's creeping me out."

Hanna moved faster, the shroud growing darker with each step. Phantom voices emerged from nowhere, whispering gibberish into her ears.

"Do you hear that?" Claire asked.

"I do. Ignore them."

The darkness continued to invade. Only a speck of the red light was visible. Everything else was pitch black. The looming voices intensified. They were no longer soft whispers, but now guttural groans of pain.

"What's happening?" Claire asked.

Hanna sensed uneasiness in her voice. "Just keep walking. We're almost there."

But they were not almost there. There was a strange sensation that they had not even moved at all. The red spotlight looked just as far as it did when they entered. The painful groans had transformed into horrifying screams, and the gust of wind was now a jet stream. Hanna felt odd pins poking at the skin on her arms.

"What the hell was that?" Claire asked. "Something touched my leg."

Hanna swiped at whatever poked her arm. "I don't know. Something's wrong. We can't stay here. We have to get to that door. Run!"

They both burst into a sprint, dashing forward as fast as they could. The steady wind pushed against them and the red spotlight was now gone, consumed by pitch black. The screams transformed again, this time into frightening growls, as if there were grotesque creatures lurking in the darkness. The poking pins suddenly felt like teeth nibbling at her arm.

"I can't see a damn thing!" Claire yelled. "Ouch! What was that?"

Hanna felt it too. The nibble had turned into a bite. "I can't see either, but it doesn't matter. It's a straight hallway. Just keep running. Don't stop!"

The growls became roars and hisses. Monstrous things were gathering around them. She couldn't see them, but she knew they were there. The monsters were watching. Tasting. Teasing. Another bite sunk into her hand. She pulled it away, in toward her chest, now running even faster. Something brushed against her leg. Something else bumped into her shoulder.

And then there was a cry of excruciating pain. It was Claire. Hanna stopped and turned around, unable to find her through the dark fog. "Claire! Are you okay?"

"It's got me! Whatever the hell this thing is, it's got me!" She let out another scream of pain.

"Extraction!" Hanna yelled. "Remember your extraction sequence." She recited the sequence out loud. "Imagine a ship sailing in the ocean." But before she could finish, a burning pain pierced her stomach. The creature had bit through her abdomen, keeping its jaw clenched. Hanna let out her own shriek of pain. Fighting the urge to pass out, she gasped for air and called out again. "Do you hear me?"

There was no answer.

"Claire, finish your extraction!"

Still no answer.

Claire was no longer there. She either successfully extracted and was back in the lab chatting with Russell, or the creature had killed her, and she was lying braindead in her chair. She prayed for the former.

But that was out of her control. She needed to focus and extract herself. She tried to ignore the pain in her stomach and ran through the sequence in her head. The ship. The waterfall. The clouds.

*****

Hanna shot up from her seat with sweat pouring down her face. Her eyes darted over to Claire's chair, where she saw Claire leaning forward with her head in her hands.

Knowing that Claire was safe, Hanna patted down her body, checking for wounds. First, she checked her stomach, where the creature had chomped down. She knew the monster was not real, but the pain had been so intense she almost expected to find a tennis ball sized hole going right through her gut.

She swiped her hand past her belly. There was no wound. Next, she inspected her arms, looking for scratch marks or pin-sized pricks, but her arms were untouched as well.

She fell back into her seat, releasing a sigh of relief.

"Christ," Russell said, rushing over to help them. "You two look awful. What happened in there?"

Claire removed her headband. "A goddamn monster attacked us."

Russell took the headband from her and hung it on the back of the chair. "Monster? What kind of monster? Is Eileen's mind really that bad?"

Hanna hung her own headband and swiveled around to sit up. "We tried to access her dorsolateral prefrontal cortex. I must have done it wrong."

"You went there without her?"

"We tried. But I think I tapped into her amygdala instead. It seems Eileen has a fear of the dark."

"Is that what that was?" Claire asked, standing up and wiping the sweat from her face. "That thing attacked us because she's afraid of the dark?"

"I've never seen such a severe case of it, but yes. That hallway exhibited telltale signs of nyctophobia."

"We barely got out alive."

"But we got out, and that's what matters. You remembered your extraction sequence and now we're safe."

Claire glanced at Eileen, who was still unconscious. "She didn't wake up. Is she okay? Did the monster get her?"

"No. She wasn't in the hallway with us. She wouldn't have been affected. It's just the sedative. It will take a while for her to wake up."

"Did you find anything?" Russell asked. "If you were trying to access her dorsolateral prefrontal cortex, I assume her memories weren't very fruitful."

"We learned a few things about Eileen's past, but nothing to help the case. We'll have to go in again to find more."

"Oh, God," Claire said. "I don't know if I can handle going back in right now."

Hanna nodded. "I agree. Not right now. First, I would like to speak with Eileen again. There are some questions I want to ask."

Russell returned to the control panel. "She'll be out for another hour or so. Passiflora is pretty strong."

"So, we'll wait. And while we wait, we can go through the case files one more time. We may have missed something."

"I would like to take another look as well," Claire said.

Hanna clapped her hands together. "Okay. Claire will come with me. Russell, keep an eye on Eileen and give us a holler when she wakes up."

Russell chuckled. "She's going to be pissed. I guess we should strap her down. I'm the one who injected her with the sedative. She might try to strangle me."

"Charles and Howard can help you with that," Claire said.

"That's right," Charles said. "Finn can give you access to the files. We'll stay here and deal with Eileen. Howard, fetch some of those extra restraints we have in the car."

Howard nodded and left the room.

"Find me when she wakes up," Hanna said. "I want to speak with her as soon as I can. We'll be in the conference room."

12: THE NAME TAG

CLAIRE AND HANNA left the lab, heading toward the conference room. As Hanna reached for the door, Finn pulled it open from the other side. "What can I do for you lovely ladies?"

"Hanna wants to take another look at the case files," Claire said.

Finn squirmed with his knees bent inward. "I would love to let you in, but I really need to use the bathroom. That iced coffee is going straight through me."

"That's fine. I can watch her."

Finn tapped his finger to the card attached to his belt. "Did you get your new security card yet?"

Claire patted her empty pockets. "Nope, not yet." She turned to Hanna. "We recently switched over to an electronic security system. Everything is done with a magnetic card. It stores electronic records to our server. So now, they know exactly who does what. I lost my card a while back, and they're taking forever to send me a new one. I have to piggyback off whoever's around." She turned back to Finn. "But you already know I have clearance. I don't mind watching her."

Finn shook his head. "Sorry, I can't give you access without that security card. SCB policy."

"Seriously, Finn? It's me. We're fine."

"I could get fired if I let you in. I'll only be gone for a few minutes. When I get back, you'll have complete access. I promise."

Claire sighed. "You're such a stickler for rules."

"Rules exist for a reason."

Hanna noticed Howard walking toward them. She waved to get his attention. "Did you find something to restrain Eileen with?"

Howard walked up with his arms crossed. "Yes. We tied her down with some high strength leather straps. There's no way she's getting out of that chair."

"Perfect timing," Finn said, shimmying in place as he spoke. "If you really can't wait for me to get back,

Howard can watch you." He poked at the card dangling from Howard's belt. "He has his security card."

Howard grinned. "Yeah, I can watch you. No problem."

"There you go," Finn said. "We all win. I'll be back in…five minutes." He peeled the name tag from his shirt and slapped it onto Howard. "Until then, Howard and I are one in the same. Now, if you'll excuse me." He trotted away with an awkward gait.

"Okay then," Howard said, opening the door. "Let's get those case files for you." He approached the safe-like box on the table and held his security card to the scanner. The cover *clicked* open, allowing him to flip through the folders inside.

Claire and Hanna sat at the end of the table. "We saw you in there," Claire said.

Howard raised his eyebrows. "You saw me in where?"

"In Eileen's memories. We saw you arrest her. Arthur and Lenny were there too."

"Yeah? That must have been weird, seeing a memory of your colleagues."

"It was definitely strange."

"You're left-handed," Hanna said. "I could tell by the way you held your gun."

He patted the holster on his left hip. "That's right."

"I'm a lefty too," she said, holding up her own left hand.

He pulled the files from the box. "It's always nice to run into another left-hander." He placed the folders on the table and slid them over.

"Thank you, Finn," Claire said, pointing her eyes at the name tag on Howard's shirt.

"He can be a real moron sometimes," Howard said. He peeled it off and slapped it down on the table.

"But he's *our* moron," Claire said with a smile.

"Yeah, well, that doesn't mean I can't still hate him for it. Anyway, don't mind me." He sat on the opposite side of the table, leaning back in his chair. "Just pretend like I'm not even here."

Hanna opened the first folder. "Okay. Let's see. Is there anything we could have missed?"

"Nothing jumps out at me," Claire said. "It's true, all three victims were fathers. And her own father physically abused her. It's a connection, but I wouldn't call it hard proof against her."

"Tony was the talkative one, right?"

"I think so. He was the one who complains about his wife."

"Okay. So, what do we know about his wife?"

Claire shrugged. "Karen? Honestly, not much. All we know is that she had a solid alibi. She was in a different state at the time of the murder. Up in Maine working a temporary job." She leaned in, squinting at one of the photos. "Man, Finn has some weird handwriting. Look at that *i*."

Hanna picked up the photo and held it closer. There was an evidence bag with a label on the front. The label read: *Eileen Warner's Hair Sample*. The vertical part of the letter *i* was slanted to the right, and the bottom swooped up to the left. "That is an odd way to write an *i*. It almost looks like a checkmark."

"Finn's an odd guy," Howard said, still leaning back in his chair with his arms crossed. "I've learned to accept his oddities. Now, I find them refreshing. As much as I tease him, he's a good guy."

"Who's a good guy?" Finn asked, entering the room.

"No one," Howard said. "They were just making fun of your handwriting."

"I know my handwriting's terrible. It's probably my greatest flaw."

"Oh, believe me," Howard said, standing up. "There are greater ones."

"Just admit it. You like me, and you know it." He glanced at his name tag, which was now stuck to the table. "What, you didn't want to roleplay as good old Finn Dooley?"

Howard walked across the room and stood in the doorway. "I may like you, but that doesn't mean I want to be you." He flashed a wink and stepped out of the room.

A grin stretched across Finn's face. "It's great, isn't it? The way we tease each other? We're like a modern-day Penn and Teller. He's Penn. I'm Teller." He tilted his head to the side. "Or maybe it's the other way around? He's Teller. I'm Penn." He crossed his arms, still unsatisfied. "Hey, Claire. Do you think I'm Penn or Teller?"

Claire shrugged. "What are you even talking about?"

"Either way, Penn and Teller are a great duo. That's what I'm getting at. We're Finn and Howard, the power team." He sat where Howard was sitting and leaned forward to peel his name tag off the table. As he pulled the corner back, the paper ripped and the *F* tore off. "Aw man, it ripped." He tried again from the opposite corner, this time tearing off the second *n* in his name, leaving only the word *in* on the table. He flicked the ripped corner into the trash. "You know what? I don't need the name tag. Everyone already knows who I am."

"It was kind of useless to begin with," Claire said. "You're the one who insisted on wearing it."

"It was for the benefit of Ms. Hanna Li, but she's learned my name by now. Isn't that right, Hanna?"

Hanna grinned. "You certainly make an impression."

"That's the best compliment I've gotten all day."

"Can we get back to the case?" Claire said, grabbing another folder and flipping it open.

Finn raised his hands over his head. "Sorry, ladies. I didn't mean to interrupt. Please, continue."

Claire pointed to a photo of Tucker Wright. "All of the victims have the same hair and eye color. Blonde hair. Blue eyes. But Eileen's father had brown hair and green eyes, like Eileen."

"What are you saying?" Hanna asked, looking at the photo of Tucker.

"We're assuming that Eileen's motive is one of revenge. She has a vendetta against men who remind her of her father. All three victims were fathers themselves, but none of them match the physical features of her own father."

Hanna slid the photo away, shaking her head. "We just don't have enough information to make any conclusions. Her memories weren't as helpful as I had hoped. We need to access her dorsolateral prefrontal cortex."

"And how do we do that? I would like to avoid another monster party."

"I'll admit, I took a risk when I tried that out. It was one I probably shouldn't have taken. We won't do that again. But we did learn a valuable nugget from the experience."

"Yeah? What's that?"

"She's afraid of the dark. In fact, I would say she's terrified of it. We can use that to our advantage."

Claire raised an eyebrow. "What are you suggesting?"

Hanna glanced at Finn, who was also listening intently. "We use it to scare her into helping us. Force her to bring us to her dorsolateral prefrontal cortex. Force her to show us the truth."

"That's pretty damn ruthless," Finn said. "Using her own fear against her like that."

"I don't actually intend to follow through, but the threat alone might be enough to persuade her."

"And if she calls your bluff?"

"Then we try something else. But it's worth a shot. Do you think Charles will approve, lying to her like that?"

Claire nodded. "Charles is incredibly enthusiastic about thought-hopping. I think he'll approve just about anything you suggest."

Russell popped his head through the door. "Eileen's awake. We've got her strapped to the chair."

"Perfect timing," Hanna said. "I want to speak with her."

"She's pretty pissed off about the sedative."

"She should be. But we're going to do it again."

Russell faked a smile. "Oh, that will be a joy."

"And she'll be even more pissed off when she hears what I have planned for her."

Claire stuffed the files back in the folders and handed them to Finn. "Thanks for your help."

Finn nodded with a salute. "Not a problem. Stop by anytime. I'll be here."

Claire and Hanna joined Russell, following him back to the lab. "What's the plan?" Russell asked.

Hanna smiled. "You'll see."

13: THE THREAT

E ILEEN SLOUCHED IN her chair, staring at Hanna with wide, furious eyes. Her nostrils flared with each heavy breath and her teeth clenched together, grinding from side to side. Thick leather straps bound her arms and legs to the chair.

"I have a few questions for you," Hanna said, sitting across from her. "Do you mind?"

Eileen sneered. "You're a pig, just like the rest of them. I knew I shouldn't have trusted you."

"I apologize for sedating you, but it was necessary. You have to understand we're only trying to help you. If you cooperate, we may be able to reduce your sentence."

She glanced at Charles, not actually sure if that statement was true. He shook his head, out of Eileen's sight.

Eileen tried to adjust her arm, but the strap prevented her from doing so. "Do you really think I'm going to believe a word you say? I can't trust anyone in this room. You're all corrupt pigs."

"I don't expect you to trust me, but I'm going to talk anyway, and I expect you to listen. We learned a few things while you were sedated. We know about your father and how he treated you. We know he physically abused you when you were a child."

"Yeah, so what?"

"It couldn't have been easy growing up like that. Getting bullied at school, and then coming home to your father."

"School sucked. Home sucked. What else is new?"

"And that's why you dropped out of school. You were a pretty good student, weren't you? But you just couldn't put up with it anymore. You threw in the towel and gave up."

"Good student? Hell no."

"Yes, you were. I saw it with my own eyes."

Eileen squinted. "What the hell does that mean?"

Hanna pointed to the headband hanging from her chair. "We were inside your mind, remember? And while we were in there, we saw all sorts of things. Thoughts.

Memories. Fears." She paused to let that last word linger. "We discovered a fear of yours while we were in there. We learned you're afraid of the dark. Is that correct?"

"Is that what you did? You found out I was scared of the dark and used it to torture me?"

Hanna flinched, caught off guard by the accusation. She intended to use Eileen's fear as a threat but, apparently, the threat had already happened. "Tell me," she said, leaning forward, "where did you end up after we sedated you? Describe it in as much detail as possible."

"I thought I was going nuts, at first, but now it all makes sense. You guys messed with my brain. Made me think I was back in Neverhill. Back on my old street. You trapped me under that goddamn light."

"We trapped you?"

"Yeah, you trapped me. I don't know how you pulled it off. Some sort of voodoo mind games, I guess. When I stepped out of the streetlight, everything went dark and that fricking monster attacked me out of nowhere. It took a bite out of my hand. Bit my pinky right off. So I went back under the light and stayed there, praying the nightmare would end. It's a sick form of torture, if you ask me."

Hanna nodded. "We'll end it, if you're willing to cooperate."

"I don't know what you want from me. I already told you I didn't do it. I didn't kill any of them. How can I make that any clearer to you morons?"

"You can lead us to your dorsolateral prefrontal cortex."

Eileen scrunched her face. "My what?"

"You can let us access the deeper parts of your brain."

"Hell no. After what you did to me last time, do you really think I'm going to let you go deeper? I don't trust you for a second. For all I know, you'll find a way to control what I say. You'll pull the strings in my brain and make me confess. Nope. There's no way I'm letting that happen."

"Then we'll continue to use your nyctophobia against you."

"My nycto-what? Look, I don't care what you do to me. The fact that you still want to poke around in my brain tells me that you haven't found what you're looking for. Otherwise, you would just send me to jail. So, as far as I'm concerned, all I have to do is sit back and let you poke because you're not going to find what you think you will."

"Okay," Hanna said. "Have fun in the dark."

She stood up and walked to where Charles, Howard, and Claire were standing. "She's not going to cooperate. She's made that clear."

"So, what now?" Charles asked.

"I didn't really expect her to cooperate, but it was worth of shot. We do have some new information, though. We know her starting location. She described her hometown. It's probably not far from where Claire and I started. And it sounds like she encountered the same monster we did."

"Can we use that against her?" Charles asked.

"We could, but I would prefer not to. I didn't intend to follow through with her nyctophobia. It was only meant to be a threat."

"Will it get results?"

"Potentially, yes. But it's torture, isn't it?"

"I don't know if you can call it torture. We're not physically harming her."

"True, nothing will physically happen to her but, mentally, she will feel pain. The experience can be just as traumatic."

"As long as she's not in physical danger, I'm okay proceeding."

"Are you sure about that?"

Charles gave a stern look. "Yes, I'm sure. Proceed with this plan. That's an order."

"Alright," Hanna said. "But not right now. We need to wait until the sedative is out of her system before we give her any more. High concentrations of sedative in her blood can be dangerous when thought-hopping, for her and us. We'll try in the morning. The footage from today's session should be processed and ready for viewing by then as well."

"Good," Charles said. "Everyone, go home and get some rest. We'll watch the footage first thing in the morning, and then we'll proceed with our second session."

Howard and Charles split off to help Russell unstrap Eileen from the chair. Hanna walked in the other direction to get her coat from her office.

Claire caught up with her in the hallway. "Do you really think this is the best plan? Torture? I can't say that I agree."

"I don't agree either," Hanna said. "But it's what Charles wants. Our job is to follow orders. Otherwise, Russell and I don't get paid."

"Our job is to get results. There must be a better way to do that."

"The only other way is to gain her trust."

"Trust? You heard her back there. She hates all of us. You were the only one she didn't despise, but you flushed that opportunity away when you told her you're working for us. You flushed it again when you decided to sedate her. There's no way she'll come back around."

Hanna shook her head. "There's always a way. We just have to find it."

14: THE PLAN

EVERYONE GATHERED AROUND the projection on the conference room wall. It was the final rendered video of Claire and Hanna navigating down the monster-ridden hallway. Most of the footage was too dark to see, but the panicked screams and haunting growls were enough to make Claire squirm in her seat.

"Are you okay?" Hanna whispered, looking over.

"I'm fine. It's just a little uncomfortable to watch. It's like we're living through it all over again. I barely got any sleep last night." Her face was pale, and there were bags under her eyes.

"Will you be okay to go back in?"

Claire pointed at the footage. "As long as we don't have to experience that again."

"There's a chance we might have to. If it's too much, I can go in by myself."

"No. This case is important and I need to do my part."

Hanna turned back to the projection. "Good. To be honest, I'm a little shaken too. After what happened, I would rather not go in alone."

The video ended, and Russell flipped on the lights. Charles stood from his seat and moved to the front of the room. He adjusted his tie and cleared his throat. "That was very interesting to see. I think this kind of footage adds incredible value to our case." He looked at Hanna and Claire. "I liked your conversation with Eileen, or what I assume to be a memory of her. It was a smart idea, but you didn't seem to get any further than we did with our own interrogations."

"Don't forget her father," Howard said. "His behavior supports her motive. She killed three fathers. Perhaps she feels that her father's death was too merciful. She believes he deserved to suffer."

"Yes," Charles said. "That's a possibility. It's still the leading theory, but we have yet to find definitive proof. We have the breadcrumbs, but we need the loaf. That's why Claire and Hanna have agreed to go back in. Hanna, would you like to brief us on your plan?"

Hanna stood up. "Yes, of course. As you all know, Eileen is unwilling to cooperate. Her cooperation is vital to accessing deeper parts of her brain. Otherwise, we could end up with those monsters again. If you haven't already figured it out, that place was her amygdala. It's where we found a manifestation of Eileen's nyctophobia. Her fear of the dark. It's a common fear, but we can use it to our advantage. If Eileen is not willing to cooperate, we can stick her inside her own amygdala. After that, she may reconsider."

Finn raised his hand. "So, your plan is to torture her?"

"Yes, in a sense. It's all in her mind, so she won't physically be harmed, but it's still potentially dangerous. If we're careful, I believe we have enough control to mitigate that danger."

"It's kind of cruel, isn't it?"

"Perhaps, but Charles wishes to proceed with this plan. We need results, and as you saw from the footage, exploring her memories has gotten us nowhere. The next logical step is to access her dorsolateral prefrontal cortex, but we need her help in order to get there. Right now, the only way to persuade her is to exploit her fear of the dark. I'm open to other suggestions, if you have them."

"What about her father?" Lenny asked from the back of the room.

"What about him?"

"He abused her when she was a child, and she's resented him ever since. You could help her confront him. That's what Core Tech Computing does, right? You use thought-hopping as a form of therapy. You help people cope with fear. Can you do the same thing with repressed hatred?"

"I suppose it's possible."

"Then that's what we do. We help her come to terms with her father. That's how we earn her trust."

"There's no way it'll work," Howard said. "We're the Serial Crimes Bureau. She thinks we're pigs."

"Hanna isn't with the bureau," Lenny said. "Sure, our little sedative incident set her back a bit, but I think Eileen is still willing to trust her under the right circumstances."

"Even if she did trust Hanna, she knows our goal is to put her in jail. Why would she help incriminate herself? She may be crazy, but she's not stupid."

Lenny stood up. "Maybe she truly believes she's not guilty. You've seen how unstable she is. She could have blacked out the murders, or just completely forgot they happened. That would explain why we couldn't find any memories. She thinks she's innocent, but if she really did kill our three victims, I would assume the truth is still in there somewhere. Right, Hanna?"

"Correct," Hanna said. "Whether she believes it or not, the truth will be in her dorsolateral prefrontal cortex. And I agree with Lenny's theory. I think she believes she's innocent. If we earn her trust, and she's confident we're not being deceptive, I think she'll cooperate. In her mind, she's not incriminating herself. She's absolving herself. Focusing on her relationship with her father is a smart move. It will elicit strong feelings of catharsis. Creating a positive experience for her is the best way to kindle her trust."

"And what if she still refuses to help?" Howard asked.

Charles stepped forward. "If she refuses, then we come up with a new plan. But I like Lenny's suggestion. It's worth trying."

"She won't play along if she thinks you're still with us," Lenny said. "You need to convince her that you're disobeying orders. Tell her that we have a plan, but instead of going along with it, you've decided to help her. Say that you believe she's innocent."

Hanna nodded. "This could work. Good job, Lenny. Let's get started."

The meeting dispersed. Hanna, Claire, Russell, and Howard headed toward the lab.

"Be honest," Howard said as they walked. "What are the chances this actually works?"

Hanna shrugged. "Not a clue."

"No offense, but based on our results so far, I just don't see this working out. Personally, I think we should pull the plug and try it the old-fashioned way. We would still pay you for your work, of course."

"I don't want to give up just yet," Claire said. "Not before we see her truth center."

Howard shook his head. "I just think we have a solid case without this stuff. We have DNA evidence."

"You already know why that's not enough."

"Let's not kid ourselves. She did it. We all know she did it. Now we're just jumping through hoops to appease the system."

"We jump through these hoops for a reason," Claire said, "The system's in place to protect the people. They're good hoops."

Howard scoffed. "Right. Good hoops."

Arthur trotted up behind them and tapped Hanna on the shoulder. "Before you start your next session, could I get in another interview? We're supposed to do one every morning."

"Yeah, sure," Hanna said. "You guys go ahead without me. This shouldn't take long."

She followed Arthur back to her office, where the tripod and camera were already set up.

"I hope you don't mind," Arthur said. "I was in here without you. I wanted to set things up first, so you don't have to watch me struggle with the camera. A whole year of using the thing, and I still haven't figured it out."

"I don't mind at all," Hanna said, circling her desk and plopping into her chair. "What kind of questions do you have for me this time? No brain-stumpers, I hope."

Arthur sat across from her, pulling out his notepad. "Nothing like that. This is more of an update interview to see where our progress stands. I guess my first question is, what is it like working with Claire? How did she do in training?"

"She did very well. She's a fast learner. Faster than most."

"In the footage this morning, she tried to save the memory of a young Eileen Warner."

"Yes, that's the one thing she hasn't quite grasped yet. Memories not being real. It speaks to her personality. She's a caring person who wants to help others in distress. I imagine it's why she was drawn to law enforcement."

"It was the same for me," Arthur said.

"It's an admirable trait, but in that particular situation, it worked against us. Sometimes it's difficult for people to understand they can't change a memory. They're events that have already happened, and they will always have the same outcome."

"Her attempt to save Eileen resulted in a struggle with her father."

"Unfortunately, it did. He didn't do any serious harm, but it's always good to avoid encounters like that."

Arthur looked down to scribble something on his notepad. When he was done, he glanced back up. "And after that, you stepped into a memory of her high school. What did you learn there?"

"We learned that she had a rough life growing up. But we already knew that. She was a victim of bullying, and she had no support system at home. She had academic potential, but a series of bad experiences pushed her toward an attempted suicide. Eventually, she dropped out of high school, and then the rest of her life fell apart."

"You had a chance to see Eileen's arrest. How was that experience for you?"

"It was definitely interesting, but I found the conversation with her leading up to that moment far more intriguing. She was a lot friendlier than when I spoke to her in person."

"Yes, she's quite unpleasant to speak to in real life."

"She was unaware the victims had died. I found that odd."

"It was pretty clear to me that she was lying. Her ignorance was an act."

"But she didn't know she was a suspect at that point. She had no reason to lie."

"If you killed someone, wouldn't you pretend like you didn't know too? Innocence through ignorance?"

"I suppose that's true, but I still think it's odd, the way she reacted."

Arthur squinted at Hanna, jotting something else on his notepad. "I disagree, but I'm not here to start an argument. For the sake of time, let's move on. Next was the hallway, or as you called it, the amygdala. From the footage, it looked quite terrifying."

"The amygdala is where the essence of your fears live. They manifest in their purest form. In Eileen's case, her fear of the dark manifests as an unseen monster. It's a classic monster in the closet scenario."

"It was too dark to see in the footage, but both of you sounded like you were in pain."

"I've tried to be transparent about this throughout the process. What happens in the mind is not physically real, but all of the sensations feel completely real, pain included."

"You said it can permanently affect your mind. Is that a concern going forward?"

"It's true, permanent damage is possible. If you're not careful, you could end up in a coma.

"That's a severe consequence. Is thought-hopping too dangerous as an investigative tool?"

"In my opinion, no. It's the same as anything else. In theory, driving a car is extremely dangerous, but if you obey the rules and stay in your lane, you'll make it to your destination without any problems. We follow the same philosophy when we're thought-hopping. We obey the rules and stay in our lane. We know what's safe and what isn't. Safety is always a priority for Core Tech Computing, and I feel safe enough to continue. I spoke with Claire, and she feels the same way."

"Fair enough," Arthur said, flipping to a fresh page and writing more. "I wanted to ask about your equipment. Yesterday, I had some time to examine your hardware. It all looks quite old."

"It's the exact same hardware we started the company with. We've wanted to upgrade for a while, but we don't have the funds."

"Are you worried that the hardware will fail while you're using it?"

"All the time. It doesn't pose a safety threat. If anything fails, we just get kicked out and wake up like normal. I'm more worried about losing data. Given the way our computer stores information, if the processor fails during a session, or the cooling fans stop and the whole system overheats, we lose that session. If the storage server fails, we have backup files in the cloud, but we would lose our ability to record anything new. The unprocessed data is just too large to store on our main hard drive."

"One of your headbands is broken too. It's one of the first things I noticed when I stepped into your lab."

"That's right. We used to have four functional headbands. To be honest, we rarely use more than two at a time. Losing one hasn't had much impact on our work. It's when we lose another that I'll start to worry."

"Is that how you intend to spend your money once your contract is complete? Upgrading your hardware?"

"It is. Our equipment is the heart of the company. Without a functional computer, Core Tech Computing doesn't exist. It's that simple. I just hope we can deliver on our end of the deal."

"Well, as long as you follow SCB rules, you should be fine. You'll get paid even if we don't get results."

"Which is very generous on your part. In a way, it takes the pressure off Russell and I but, at the same time, I feel more obligated to find something useful for your case."

"Are you confident in your ability to do that?"

Hanna paused to think about the question. "Before we started, I was unsure, but now that we've had our first session, I'm more confident. The dangers are more manageable than I expected. And while we didn't find what we were looking for in her memories, I have no doubt we'll find it in her dorsolateral prefrontal cortex. We just have to convince her to take us there, and I believe we have a solid way of doing that. Once she lets us in, we can finally know the truth. Hopefully, that happens today."

"Very good," Arthur said, flipping his notepad shut. "That wraps up our second interview. You're free to catch up with the others in the lab. Thank you for your time."

"Of course," Hanna said, standing up. "I look forward to the next one."

"Tomorrow morning. Same time. Same place. It will hopefully be an exit interview, if all goes well today."

"Fingers crossed," she said, opening the door and leaving the room.

When she reached the lab, Eileen was screaming and tugging at her restraints. "You can all go to hell!" Her body jolted back and forth, trying to jostle free. "You're corrupt pigs. Every one of you. Punishing an innocent woman to make a quick buck in Hollywood. You make me sick."

Russell was at the control panel booting up the computer. "Howard, get the sedative. And remember, not the Temazepam. You're looking for Passiflora."

When Eileen heard the word *sedative*, she stopped yelling and lowered her voice. "Please, don't put me under. I beg."

Hanna walked over and whispered in her ear. "I'm here to help. I promise." She looked up at Howard, who had found the sedative and held the syringe. "Do it."

Howard plunged the needle into her arm. Her violent thrashing melted away as she fell into a deep sleep. Claire sat in the same spot beside her.

Russell left the control panel to help with the headbands, but Claire grabbed her own and put it on herself. "I got it. I've done this enough times to know how it goes."

"Okay," Hanna said. "We're good to go."

"Be careful in there," Russell said, moving back to the control panel. "Her nyctophobia looked nasty in that video. Keep an eye on each other, and if anything goes wrong, don't be afraid to extract. I'll be ready to pull you out."

"We'll be fine," Hanna said. "As long as we stick to the plan, everything should be okay."

15: THE SONG

CLAIRE AND HANNA appeared on the same street in Neverhill. It was still night. All of the lights were still off. All of the houses were still dark. And the glowing moon was still the only source of light. Further down the street, there was the same cul-de-sac they had seen before.

"Now, we just need to find Eileen," Hanna said, turning to look the other way. The road stretched to the horizon with no apparent end. "This time, we walk this way."

"How do we find her?" Claire asked, walking beside her.

"I spoke with her yesterday. She told me that after we sedated her, she appeared in Neverhill." Hanna gestured to the houses around them. "This is Neverhill. So, we walk until we find her. She shouldn't be far."

There was a distant scream, just barely audible.

"What was that?" Claire asked.

They stopped, staring at each other with their ears turned. There was another scream from what sounded like only a few blocks away.

"That's her," Hanna said. "Remember the plan. She needs to think we're disobeying orders. They sent us in here to torture her, but we're actually here to help."

They jogged along the empty road, coming across a four-way intersection. Straight ahead, the road stretched infinitely. To the right and left, the same thing. They stood at the center of the intersection, waiting for another scream.

When it came, they turned left and dashed toward the hollering voice. They passed rows of identical houses. The same blue door. The same white vinyl siding. The same brick chimney. Over and over. House after house. Eileen's voice grew louder. Clearer. Closer. Until they finally reached another cul-de-sac, and at the opposite end of the circle, standing on the concrete sidewalk, was Eileen.

She squeezed her arms around her body, trembling as sweat dripped from her face. She stood under the only working streetlight, which shined with blinding intensity. A low but audible hum buzzed from the bulb as it cast down a ray of light.

Before she could let out another scream, she noticed Claire and Hanna standing across from her. "No," she mumbled. "Not you. Anyone but you."

"It's okay," Hanna said, approaching with caution. "We're here to help."

"Get away from me." She backed away, stepping out of the light, and as she did, the sky darkened. The moonlight faded. The frightening growls emerged. "Oh, no," she said, scrambling back into the light. The growls silenced, and the sky returned to normal. She stood still and held her palm toward them. "Stay back. Don't come any closer. I don't need any more trouble."

"We're not here to bring trouble," Hanna said. "I told you, we're here to help."

"Why would you help me?"

"Because I believe you're innocent."

Eileen's eyes widened. "You what?"

"She believes you're innocent," Claire said. "And so do I."

"You're still the prime suspect," Hanna said. "At least according to the SCB. They sent us in here to use your fear of the dark against you, but we're not going to do that."

Eileen flipped her hair back. "Why the change of heart? Yesterday, you threatened me, and now you want to help?"

"We think there was an error with the evidence, but none of the others believe us. Right now, we're working independently of the SCB. None of them know what we're really doing in here."

"They can't see us?"

"They cannot. This conversation is private. They can't see or hear anything we do."

"But she knows," Eileen said, pointing at Claire. "She's with the SCB. She'll tell them."

"No," Hanna insisted. "We can trust her."

"I don't even know if I can trust you. You drugged me up and trapped me under this light."

Hanna glanced at the lightbulb above. "You're trapped?"

"That's what I said. When I step out, that monster comes back, so I'm stuck standing here alone in the middle of the night. I hate being outside at night. It freaks me out."

"You're afraid of the dark. It's your mind's way of manifesting your fear. You can leave, but you have to confront your fear."

"That creature bit off my pinky last time." She shook her head. "Nope. Nah-uh. I'm not letting that happen again. I'll stay right here until I wake up. I hate standing under this goddamn light, but it's better than being eaten alive."

"We saw your father," Claire said.

Eileen tilted her head. "You what? How is that possible?"

Claire stepped forward and leaned against the base of the light. "We saw him in one of your memories. We know what he used to do to you."

"The man was a coward," Eileen said. "He didn't deserve an ounce of respect. I only wish I had realized that sooner. I spent my entire childhood fearing the man. If I could see him now, I would tell him how worthless he is."

"You deserved better."

"Do you think I wanted the life I ended up with? Of course not. But what other choice did I have? Sure, I did well in school, but he didn't support a single thing I did. I wasn't going to college. I had no future. He wouldn't have let me." She glanced at her feet. "If I could see him one more time. Tell him he's trash. Show him how much better off I am without him."

"You can," Hanna said. "We can bring you to a memory of him, and you can say whatever you want."

"Why would you do that for me? What's in it for you?"

"I don't want to see an innocent woman go to jail. I want to clear your name, and to do that, we need you to bring us to your dorsolateral prefrontal cortex. It's where your truths are stored. If you're innocent, which I believe you are, we should find definitive proof there. It's a very personal part of the brain and you should only bring us there if you trust us completely. I realize you may not be there with us yet, but we would like an opportunity to earn back some of that trust."

"So, you bring me to my father, and then I bring you to this dorso place?"

"If you trust us, yes. But first, we have to get you away from this streetlight."

Eileen looked down at the perimeter of light around her. "What about the monster?"

"This is your mind. You have control. If you focus on overcoming your fear, the monster won't hurt you."

Eileen inhaled through her nose and released it through her mouth, stepping closer to the edge of the light. Her second step crossed the threshold into the dark. The sky dimmed and a dark mist overcame them. The ominous whispers returned, speaking nonsense in a low, grumbling tone.

Hanna swiveled her head around, watching the shroud of darkness invade. "Focus, Eileen. Don't let your fear overwhelm you."

Eileen took another step, this one bringing her completely out of the light. The world darkened more as the eerie cloud consumed them. The grumbling whispers transformed into growls, a noise Claire and Hanna both dreaded.

Hanna could not see the creature through the dense fog, but she could feel it brush against her leg. "You have to focus, Eileen."

"I am focusing, goddamn it. It's not working. And that fricking monster is back. I can't do this. I'm going back." She spun around to return to safety, but the streetlight had turned off. Now, there was only darkness. "It's not there. The goddamn light is gone."

"Stay calm. Panicking will only make it worse." The growls transformed into roars, and she could feel the pricks and pins on her hand.

"How can I stay calm when the only thing that's been keeping me safe has disappeared? This is your fault. I should have ignored you and just stayed under the light."

There was a nibble on Hanna's leg. "Please. You have to stay calm."

"Stop saying that!"

Hanna could no longer see Eileen or Claire. The darkness had engulfed everything. She could barely even see her own body. A set of sharp teeth poked at her skin, ready to chomp at any moment. She prepared for the unbearable pain that would come once the creature decided to take another bite out of her torso. Eileen was not in control, and things were about to get very dangerous. It was time to give up. "Claire!" she yelled. "Extract!"

She waited for an answer, but did not receive one. Another set of teeth scratched against her arm, puncturing her skin. There was no more time. She had to get out. She recited the sequence in her head. The ship. The water. The clouds. She was nearly done, but then she paused, hearing Claire's voice.

Claire was singing "Love Me Tender," the delightful Elvis tune they had heard on the CD player. Her melodic voice was soft and soothing. There were many words to describe her singing, but for Hanna, only one came to mind: angelic.

The sharp teeth disappeared. The guttural growls subsided. The night sky returned to its normal moon-lit hue. Eileen stood in front of the curb, staring at Claire with entranced eyes. She mouthed the lyrics as Claire sang them, swaying her head to the soothing tempo.

"That song," Eileen said. "I've loved that song ever since I was a child. Whenever I had the chance, I would flip on the old black and white videos of Elvis. I loved all of his songs, but that one was always my favorite."

Claire reached the end of the song and smiled. "You did it. You're in the dark, and there's no monster. You're not trapped anymore."

A surprised smile crept onto Eileen's face. "Would you look at that?"

"You did well," Hanna said. "I'm sorry I pushed you."

Eileen shrugged. "It got me out. So, thank you, I guess."

"You're welcome. Now, let's find your father."

Eileen turned around and stared at the house in front of them. A light in the window flickered on. "Right, my father."

16: THE GLITCH

THE THREE OF them stared at the blue door. Hanna reached for the doorknob, but Eileen stopped her. Her hands were clammy and trembled.

"I don't know about this," she said.

Hanna looked into her eyes. "This is what you want, right? This is important to you?"

"I thought it was, but I never thought I would get the chance. I didn't think I would ever see him again. Now that we're here, I don't know."

"You're nervous. That's normal. It means you care."

"I haven't seen him in over ten years. What do I say?"

"Whatever feels right. Tell him everything you told us. Let him know how you feel. Say everything you never had a chance to say before he died. And remember, this is about you. Not him."

Eileen took a deep breath and nodded. "Okay. I'm ready."

Hanna turned the doorknob and the three of them entered the house. They stood in the same living room as before, but instead of a young Eileen on the couch, it was her father watching television. He aimed the remote at the glowing box, flipping from channel to channel.

Claire and Hanna stepped aside, clearing a path for Eileen.

"Dad," Eileen said, inching forward.

Her father looked up. "Eileen, I told you not to bother me while I'm watching TV." He turned his attention back to the screen.

"Dad," she said again.

This time, he ignored her. She walked around the couch and stood between him and the television.

"What the hell are you doing, child?" He stood up and chucked the remote at her.

She blocked the projectile and stomped forward. "I'm not a child anymore, Dad. I've grown up."

He rolled his eyes. "Whoop-de-fricking-doo. What, do you want an award? News flash, lady. We all get old. It's not a fricking talent."

"Don't call me lady. I'm your daughter."

"Oh, yeah? Then tell me, what did my good-for-nothing daughter grow up to be?"

Eileen broke eye contact, looking at her feet. "I'm a prostitute," she whispered.

"What did you say? Speak up, girl, and don't goddamn mumble."

"I said I'm a prostitute."

He nodded. "So, that's your crowning achievement. You have sex for money. It figures. I knew you wouldn't amount to much."

"It's because of you," she said.

"Because of me? What the hell did I have to do with this? You can't blame me. If anything, I should be pissed at you. You've tainted the family name. Now people will remember me as the father of the fricking prostitute. Goddamn and Christ almighty, I can't even catch a break when I'm dead."

"You always make it about yourself. The universe doesn't revolve around you. You're not the center of everything."

"Come on. You do the same thing. A couple of kids tease you at school, and you completely blow it out of proportion. But it turns out, you're not even good at slitting your own wrists."

"I was a child, and you were my father. You're supposed to comfort your daughter when she comes home weeping. You don't yell at her. You don't call her a whore like the rest of them."

"But look at you now. You've become a professional whore. The prophecy has come true."

"You're not listening to me. You never do. It's your fault I dropped out of high school. It's your fault I tried to kill myself. And it's your goddamn fault they think I'm a murderer."

He smiled. "That's right, I almost forgot. You're wanted for murder. Tell me, did you do it?"

Eileen stared at him, refusing to answer.

"Come on, you can tell me. I'm you're father. Did you really stab Tony eighty-eight times? That's just ruthless."

"You know I didn't do it."

"To be frank, I really don't care whether you did it or not. What I care about is the fact that you *could* do it. We both know you have blood on your hands. You killed your own mother."

"I didn't kill her. She died when I was a baby."

"She died giving birth to you."

"You can't blame me for that."

"I can, and I do. I always have. And when she died, I was stuck with an ungrateful brat. She didn't deserve to die. She was an angel. If I could trade your life for hers, I would do it in an instant."

Eileen flinched. "Don't say that. Take it back."

"I will not take it back. It's the truth. You're the one thing that ruined my life."

"No. Take it back."

"You're a curse. You're the goddamn mistake. You stole your mother from me."

She pounded on his chest with her fists. "Take it back! Take it back! Take it back!"

"No!" he yelled, shoving her away.

She tripped over the coffee table and tumbled over. When she hit the floor, she rolled over and scurried to the wall. "Please, it's not true."

"Not true?" he repeated, looking down at her as he walked forward. He undid his belt, pulling it from the waist of his pants and folding it in half. "Are you calling me a liar? As far as I can tell, you're the only one who's lying. And guess what. Liars need to be taught a lesson." He raised the belt over his head to strike her.

Claire lunged forward, crashing into his side and knocking him to the floor. He landed on a pile of pizza boxes, shaking his head, and fluttering his eyes in a daze.

Claire hopped up and crouched beside Eileen, offering a hand. "Are you okay?"

Eileen stared back at her in awe. "I still don't get it. Why are you helping?"

"I told you, I believe you're innocent."

A wooden bat slammed into the side of Claire's head. She dropped to the floor, bouncing off a wall on her way down. The man stood behind her, winding up for another swing.

Hanna charged forward, lifting the man up by the waist and throwing him onto the kitchen table. Empty beer bottles smashed under his weight, sending shards of glass through the air.

He pushed her away and hopped off the table to wind up another swing. Hanna raised her arms and caught the bat as it came down. She yanked it from his hands and jabbed his gut with the handle.

He keeled over, clenching his stomach, but recovered with an unexpected burst of strength. He lifted her up by the legs and slammed her down on the floor, sending the bat out of her hands and knocking the breath from her lungs. She squirmed on the floor, gasping for air as the man sat on top of her, straddling her stomach.

He raised his fist and smashed it into her face. A burst of stars invaded her vision. She tried to lift him off, but another fist caught her cheek, draining all of the strength from her body. Her arms fell limp to her sides, too exhausted to fight back anymore. Anticipating a third punch, she turned her head away.

Claire ran over and kneed him in the temple. He flopped over, landing beside the wooden bat. He fumbled to pick it up, when Eileen walked over and snatched it away.

He glared up at her, letting out a nervous laugh. "Hold on there, honey. You wouldn't hurt your own father, would you? You're not the monster they say you are. You're my girl. My daughter. My princess."

"Cut the crap," Eileen said. "You're just as pathetic as I remember. You never supported me when I needed you most. I'm glad you're out of my life."

His laugh turned maniacal. "Crazy bitch. You'll never amount to anything. You're a whore, and you'll die a whore. You'll piss off a client, and he'll shoot you in the head. He'll put you down like the dog you are."

She lined up the end of the bat with the top of his head and wound up her swing. "Burn in hell."

The bat slammed down, crushing his skull. His body went limp, and he crumpled over.

Eileen let the weapon roll out of her hand, wiping the tears from her face. "Thank you. Both of you."

Claire patted the dust from her shirt. "I wasn't going to let him hurt you."

"We know what you've been through," Hanna said. "We saw the relationship you had with your father. We wanted to give you a chance to confront him."

The man's body vanished in front of them.

"He's gone," Eileen said.

Hanna guided her toward the front door. "That's right. You stood up to him. Now, he's gone for good."

Claire opened the door and escorted her out of the house. Hanna followed, glancing back to see Eileen's father reappear on the couch, flipping through channels on the television. "Gone for good," she repeated. She stepped outside and shut the door.

"I was wrong about the two of you," Eileen said. "You're decent people. I'll take you wherever you want to go."

"Good," Hanna said. "But remember, when you wake up, pretend like you despise us. The rest of the SCB thinks we tortured you."

"That's easy enough. I excel in despising people. So, you want me to take you to this truth place?"

"Yes. It's called the dorsolateral prefrontal cortex."

"Honey, I ain't calling it that. It's called the truth place." She glanced around at the identical houses. "How do I take you there? Which one of these—"

Time hiccupped as she finished her sentence, pausing for a moment, and then skipping ahead.

"What was that?" Claire asked, twisting her head in confusion.

Hanna rubbed her chin. "I don't know. That's never happened bef—"

Another hiccup cut her off. She looked at her hands, which were fading away. Claire and Eileen were transparent as well.

"What's going on?" she muttered to herself. "Claire, are you seeing th—"

Before she could finish, there was one last hiccup, and then everything went dark.

*****

Hanna woke up in the lab, confused and disoriented. She turned her head to check on Claire and Eileen. Claire was also awake, squinting as her eyes adjusted to the light. Eileen was still unconscious.

"What happened?" Hanna asked, removing her headband.

Russell mashed at the keys on the keyboard. "I have no idea." All of the monitors shut off at once. He stopped what he was doing and stared at the blank screens. The computer emitted a loud extended *beep*, and then shut down.

"No," Hanna said, hopping out of her seat and scurrying over to the giant machine. "Please, no."

"Is this normal?" Charles asked, watching from the back. "Does this happen a lot?"

"No, this isn't normal," Russell said, leaving the control panel to join Hanna. "Did it die?"

"I really hope not," she said, pressing her hand to the side of the case. "It's hot." She leaned back and pointed to the counter next to Claire. "Can you hand me the screwdriver?"

"Sure thing," Claire said. She searched the area for a screwdriver. "Where is it?"

"There should be one on the counter."

"Well, it's not here. All I see is a boxcutter."

"Throw that over. That should work."

Claire tossed the boxcutter across the room. Hanna caught it and used the tip of the blade to unscrew the fasteners along the edge of the case.

"See?" Russell said. "The boxcutter is always useful."

She removed the side panel and placed it on the floor, already feeling the heat emanate from within. "Why is it so hot?"

"Look," Russell said, pointing to the back of the machine. "The cooling fans are unplugged from the power supply."

Hanna could see the loose wires dangling freely. "How did that happen? I can see maybe one of them coming loose, but not all of them at the same time."

Russell shrugged. "Who knows? Anything's possible, I guess." He plugged the cords back in. "There we go. All fixed up."

Charles stepped closer to peek inside the case. "Can you continue the session from where you left off?"

"We can't do anything until it cools down," Russell said. "We'll have to wait. I don't want to risk any permanent damage."

"But you will be able to continue once it's cooled down?"

"We should be able to, assuming no damage is already done. It's an old computer. This kind of thing can put a lot of stress on the processor."

"If there is damage," Hanna said, walking across the room to talk directly to Charles, "our investigation is over. I'm afraid this is our only system. We have no backups. We'll know for sure once the temperature stabilizes."

"How long until we can start it up again?"

"An hour. But like yesterday, we shouldn't overdo the sedatives. We can test the equipment to make sure everything is working properly, but until the sedative is out of Eileen's system, we shouldn't go back in. Tomorrow morning is safer."

"Will it save today's footage?"

"It should," Russell said. "We store all of the raw data on this external storage server." He patted the plastic box on the counter. "We can't process the data until the computer has cooled down, but all of it is saved on this box."

Charles nodded. "Good. Tomorrow morning we'll continue from where we left off. How did today's session go before the glitch? Did you make any progress?"

"We did," Hanna said. "A lot of progress, actually. Our plan worked. She thinks we're working against the SCB. We've gained her trust and she's agreed to cooperate. I think we'll get results tomorrow."

"Excellent news," Charles said.

Howard stroked the stubble on his chin, watching Hanna. "You sound confident."

"I am confident. For once, things are going our way." She glanced at the overheated computer. "For the most part."

"Okay, folks," Charles said. "No more thought-hopping for today." He turned back to Hanna. "If it's okay with you, I would like to work in your building for the rest of the day. It'll save us a drive back to SCB Headquarters. We'll be out of your hair in the evening."

"Yes, of course," Hanna said. "Make yourselves at home."

She glanced at Eileen, who was waking up from her slumber. Her eyes opened, squinting under the bright lights. She searched the room, twisting her head around until she found Hanna. They locked eyes, and with the exchange of a subtle nod, they confirmed their agreement. Eileen adjusted her posture, snorted, and then shouted at the top of her lungs.

"You pigs will never break me! You call that torture? You're embarrassing yourselves. No wonder the SCB's reputation is in the gutter. This is how you investigate? Pathetic." She turned to Claire, who stood beside her. "You make me sick."

"There goes my peace and quiet for the day," Russell said, walking back to his seat.

Claire patted his shoulder. "You'll miss her when she's gone."

"I highly doubt that." He spun in his chair to face Eileen. "No offense."

Eileen flashed an ugly face.

"Good luck with her," Claire said, leaving the room with Hanna.

They walked side by side down the hallway together.

"She truly believes she's innocent, doesn't she?" Claire asked.

Hanna shrugged. "Maybe she is."

"Do you really think that?"

"I don't know what to think anymore. All I know is that there's no other reason for her to cooperate. Either she's telling the truth, or she has something else planned."

"Like what?"

"We're lying to her to gain her trust. Maybe she's doing the same thing. She could be leading us into a false sense of security, and when she finds the right opportunity, she'll pull the carpet right out from under our feet."

Claire scrunched her face. "Now that I think about it, we did just set her free. She couldn't hurt us when she was trapped under that light, but now she can do whatever she wants."

"That's right. It's her mind. She has control. I don't think she realizes how much power that gives her. If she figures it out, we could be in a lot of trouble. Although, the more likely scenario is that she loses control altogether and throws us all into unfathomable danger."

"Let's just hope it doesn't come to that. I'm sure everything will go exactly as planned. She'll bring us to her truth center, and by the end of tomorrow, this case will be closed."

"You make it sound so easy."

Claire shrugged. "Who knows? Maybe it will be."

"Nothing's ever easy."

17: THE LETTER

HANNA PEERED THROUGH the window, watching Claire drive out of the parking lot, followed by Howard and Charles. Lenny and Arthur were stuffing Eileen in the back seat of their sedan. They would bring her to the same motel they had been staying at for the last two nights.

Russell was still with her in the lab, shutting down the computer. "I'm so relieved everything still works," he said. "That fan incident gave me a scare."

Hanna left the window and walked over to the computer, running her fingers along the side panel of the case. "Me too. Let's make sure that never happens again. We've had enough hardware issues."

"The diagnostic tests say everything is back to normal. We should be fine, as long as no one unplugs the cooling fans."

"Was it just a loose connection?"

"It's possible, I guess, but the cords click in. I have a hard time believing all of them just slipped out on their own."

"I've got a weird feeling about this," Hanna said, staring straight ahead. "And it's not just the cooling fans. Something's off about this case."

"Don't stress about it. Tomorrow, we'll get inside her dorsolateral prefrontal cortex. We'll find the evidence we need and finally get that big paycheck we deserve. Core Tech Computing will live on, and life will continue as it was. Just go home and get some sleep. We'll wrap this up in the morning."

"I don't know if I'll be able to sleep. Maybe I'll stay late and look through the case files again."

"You can't look at the case—"

"I know," Hanna interrupted, rolling her eyes. "I can't look at the case files without SCB supervision. Finn is still here, right?"

"I think so. But you better hurry. I saw him packing up. And don't stay too late. It's supposed to snow later tonight."

"Thanks, Russell," she said, backstepping out of the lab. "Get some rest."

She strolled down the hall, catching Finn just as he was shutting the door to the conference room.

He waved. "Have a good night. See you in the morning."

"Wait," she said. "I was hoping to take another look at the case files."

"Sorry. No can do. I've got a leftover pizza waiting for me back home." He patted his stomach. "There's something about this case that really burns those calories right out of you. I've got to replenish. Otherwise, I'll be all skin and bones."

Hanna glanced at his slim belly. "Russell's the same way. He eats and eats, but no matter how much he stuffs down his mouth, he's as thin as a stick. He says he's Pac-Man, and I'm the snake.

"The snake?" Finn asked.

"You know, that game that came with every computer back in the day. You eat an apple, and the snake grows, but Pac-Man eats all of the fruit in the world and doesn't grow an inch."

"I don't think that metaphor works."

"Yeah, Russell was never great with metaphors."

"At least Pac-Man has some heft to him. Just look at these arms." He rolled up his sleeve to show her. "Twigs.

You want a video game metaphor? You're Mike Tyson, and I'm Glass Joe."

"Some people would kill to have that problem."

"Yeah, well, I would kill to have a little muscle. Hell, I'd settle for King Hippo at this point."

"Okay, take it easy, Mr. Punch-Out. I didn't mean to strike a nerve. I was just hoping you would stay a little longer. I really wanted to look at those files. I won't be long."

"You know, in my entire career, I've never stayed a minute later than I've had to." He glanced at his watch. "I'd hate to break that streak."

"You don't have to stay. Just leave your security card with me. I'll pack everything up when I'm done."

"You know I can't do that. It's against SCB policy. I could lose my job. And you would be in violation of your contract. If anyone found out, you would lose your big paycheck."

She shrugged. "Yeah, I know. It was worth a shot."

"I'll let you see them first thing in the morning. I promise."

"If you stay late, I'll buy you a fresh pizza from the place of your choosing. Piping hot, right out of the oven. None of this day-old fridge pizza nonsense."

Finn's ears perked up. "How can I turn down a deal like that? I guess the infamous streak ends today. I'll give you ten minutes, but that's it." He dug into his pocket, searching for the security card. "Hmm," he mumbled. "Where did I put it?" He patted the back of his pants. Nothing. He peeked into his breast pocket. Still nothing. "I must have misplaced it. I wish I could help, but I can't open that box without my card. I'll find it in the morning, or Howard can give you access when he gets in. That's the best I can do."

"Are you sure you can't help? You're giving up your pizza just like that?"

"What do you want me to do, break the damn safe open with my hands? Need I remind you?" He rolled up his sleeve again. "Twigs. Besides, some people consider cold pizza a delicacy."

Hanna sighed. "I guess I can wait. But I'm going to find you first thing in the morning."

Finn pointed finger guns at her. "I'm looking forward to it." He turned around and walked away. "Have a good night, Hanna. Go home. Get some sleep."

She stood alone in the hallway, watching him turn the corner. Once he was gone, she cupped her hands around her eyes and pressed against the viewing window in the door. The room was dark, but the blinking red light of the overhead projector provided just enough light to see.

The box-shaped safe was on the table, tethered to one of the legs with a metal strap. An assortment of crumpled chip bags and candy wrappers surrounded Finn's seat at the head of the table.

She stared at the pile of wrappers, watching them light up whenever the projector light flashed. They illuminated like red stars in the vast void of outer space. And out of that void, away from the wrappers, she noticed another object reflecting the red light. It was a piece of plastic on the floor beneath the chair.

"Hmm," Hanna mumbled. She entered the room and flipped on the lights, circling around the table, keeping her eye on the piece of plastic. She bent down to pick it up, studying the portrait of Finn. It was his security card.

In the photo, his hair was unusually long, draping down in front of his face. Instead of a professional shirt and tie, he wore a baggy pullover hoodie. There was bold text printed next to the photo: *Finn Dooley - Security Level 2.*

She shook her head and grinned. "Finn Dooley, you're a messy, disorganized slob, and I love you for it."

The sound of a car motor came from the window. She walked over to peer out at the parking lot. Russell's car was already gone and Finn was pulling out of his spot. The only car left was her own. She watched Finn drive away, and once he was gone, she scurried back across the room to close the door. With the security card in her hand, she approached the safe.

The scanner was near the top of the box, just below the handle. She glanced at the card again, this time reading the fine print on the back. *This card is to be used by the cardholder and no one else.* Did she really want to break the rules? Was it worth the risk?

The future of Core Tech Computing was at stake, but there was something about this case that twisted her gut in all the wrong ways. Something was horribly wrong, and she needed to figure out what it was. The office was empty. No one else was around. She would take a look, find what she needed, lock the files back up, and place Finn's card back where she found it. No one would ever know.

In a wavering moment of self-doubt, she placed the card on the table and stared at it. Eileen's face appeared in her mind. The expression she had after confronting her father. It was the face of someone tormented by a lifetime of abuse, both physical and emotional. It was the face of someone who had attempted suicide after enduring the cruelty of high school bullying. It was the face of someone who had given up her academic future in favor of prostitution. It was a saddened face, but not the face of a killer.

"Screw it," she muttered, picking up the card and holding it in front of the scanner.

There was a soft *click* as the locking mechanism released. She opened the top and pulled out the folders, spreading the contents across the table. With the papers laid out, she skimmed through all of the information, hoping to find something new.

The first murder. Anthony Higgs. Stabbed eighty-eight times in his house in Roxbury. Girlfriend was in Maine. Two-year-old daughter was found alive upstairs.

The second murder. Cameron Shultz. Stabbed fifty-four times in his house in Dorchester. No signs of struggle. Wife was at work. Two daughters were at school. Back door was kicked in.

The third murder. Tucker Wright. Stabbed sixty-one times in his apartment in Mattapan. Girlfriend was at her sister's house. Son and daughter were at his ex-wife's house. Found by maintenance worker. Door was unlocked. No sign of a break in.

None of it was helpful. If Eileen was innocent, who else could it be? At one point, the wife and two girlfriends had been primary suspects. The three murders were considered unrelated domestic homicides carried out by disgruntled partners. But there was no evidence to incriminate any of them. They all had solid alibis.

The only connection between the three victims was their relationship with Eileen. And to close it all out, Eileen's hair was found at all three crime scenes. It was the strongest evidence against her and the reason she was in SCB custody.

Hanna flipped from the victim profiles to the crime scene evidence. The murder weapons were not identical. Three separate kitchen knives taken from three separate homes. No fingerprints. No signs of struggle, other than the kicked in door.

She leaned closer to study the photo of the broken door frame. *No signs of struggle.* That's what the report said, but how could the perpetrator kick in the door without startling the victim? Certainly, there would have been an altercation if Eileen had kicked in the door and attacked him with a knife. But analysis of the crime scene showed no struggle at all. Apparently, Mr. Shultz had ignored the door blasting open and decided to continue eating his breakfast.

Unless the person had killed him first and kicked it open after. Someone with a key to the house who wanted to make it look like a break-in. Eileen knew Cameron Shultz, but did she know him well enough to have a key to their house? Hanna doubted it.

He could have invited her in. His kids were at school and his wife was away. Inviting her into his house was plausible. Then she killed him, panicked, and kicked the door to cover her tracks. But Eileen didn't visit her clients in their homes. That's not how she operated. They always came to her.

Leaving that thought, Hanna shifted her focus to a photo of Eileen's hair. It was the one piece of evidence that was hardest to dispute. Hairs were found on the clothes of each victim. An argument could be made that it was just coincidence, that the hair had migrated, but it was unlikely. A single load of laundry would have cleaned any hair right out. No matter how much she nitpicked the rest of the evidence, the hair pointed right back at Eileen Warner.

Hanna leaned back, rubbing her eyes. There was nothing else to see. She was trying to defend someone who was probably guilty. It was time to give up and go to sleep. She shuffled the papers back into place and slid them into the safe.

As she reached for the cover, her eyes caught the name tag that was still stuck to the surface of the table. It was the same name tag that Howard had slapped down. The same name tag Finn had ripped while trying to peel it off. He had torn off the *F* and the second *n*, but the middle part of his name was still intact. She squinted to focus on the letter *i*.

"Hold on a minute," she said to herself.

Her heart raced as she grabbed the folder and flipped through the pages. When she found the three photos of

Eileen's hair, she placed them side by side, leaning forward with her face only inches from the table. Each hair sample was held in an evidence bag, and each bag had a handwritten label: *Eileen Warner's Hair Sample.*

She recalled pointing out the peculiar handwriting to Claire. Specifically of the letter *i*. The vertical part was slanted to the right and the bottom swooped up to the left. Like a checkmark. She had never seen an *i* written like that before, but there it was. In the words *Eileen* and *hair*, both swooped to the left. She glanced back at Finn's name tag. No swoop.

She flipped through photos of other evidence. The murder weapons. The victims. The crime scenes. All had labels that matched the handwriting on Finn's name tag. All except the hair samples.

Finn was the only one processing the crime scene. He was the only one bagging evidence and taking photos. And he was supposed to be the only one writing labels. But now there was a second set of handwriting, and the only place it appeared was on the three pieces of evidence that linked Eileen to the murders. Someone other than Finn had planted the bags of hair. Eileen was being framed.

A muffled sound came from the hallway. Hanna jumped in her seat. Her eyes darted to the viewing window in the door, but it was too dark to see if anyone was in the hallway.

She froze, keeping her eye on the window. The darkness remained for a moment longer, and then a dim light turned on. Someone had returned to the office, and she was looking at classified government files without the proper supervision. She stumbled around the table, stuffing everything back in the safe. She closed the top, and as soon as the lock clicked, she tossed Finn's security card onto the floor.

Mindful of the sound she was making, she tiptoed to the door and cracked it open, peeking through the thin slit. The corridor was mostly dark, illuminated only by a light around the corner. The light was coming from the lab. Had Russell forgotten something and returned to retrieve it?

"Russell?" she called out, leaving the conference room, and wading through the hallway. "Is that you?"

There was no answer. As she passed the kitchen, she glanced at the clock on the wall. Eight o'clock. She had lost track of time. Who would come back to the office so late?

She turned the corner and entered the lab, finding a man standing at the control panel, facing away from her. He wore a black hood over his head and dark leather gloves.

"Russell?" she said, glaring at the back of his head. "What's with the outfit?"

The man spun around, freezing in place when he saw her. His face was obscured by a black ski mask.

Filled with panic, Hanna searched for a weapon. On the counter was Russell's boxcutter. She picked it up and pushed out the blade, holding it in front of her. "Who are you? What are you doing here?"

The man did not answer. Not a word. Not a noise. Nothing. He stood with his arms at his sides, staring back at her.

Hanna was paralyzed with doubt. She had a weapon, but the man was large. He could easily overpower her. She stepped forward and raised the blade higher. "I asked you a question. Who are you?"

Again, no response. He moved his hand to his waist.

"Hey!" Hanna yelled, stepping forward again. "Don't move a muscle."

He ignored her, lifting the bottom of his shirt to reveal a holster clipped to his belt. He drew his gun and aimed at her head.

She stopped advancing and retracted the blade, raising her hands over her head. "Okay, I'm backing off. No need to escalate things any further. All I want to do is talk. What do—"

Before she could finish, the man holstered his weapon, spun around, and grabbed the storage server from the counter. He yanked out the wires and sprinted across the room.

18: THE CHASE

WITH A HANDFUL of wires dangling behind him, the intruder ran to the end of the lab and slammed through the closed door.

"Hey!" Hanna yelled. "Stop!" She stuffed the boxcutter into her pocket and bolted across the room, following him through the door and into the stairwell.

The *clop* of his shoes echoed off the bare concrete walls as he scurried down the steps. Hanna leaned over the railing, watching the top of his hood spiral down the stairs. She followed him down, skipping every other step and bursting into the empty lobby.

The receptionist was gone and the security guards had finished their shift. She ran through the vacant room and plowed past the front doors.

The frigid air slapped her face and smoky clouds escaped her mouth. Snowflakes drifted down from the sky and a thin coat was forming on the ground. She swiveled her head back and forth, searching for the intruder.

To her left, there were Harvard University dorms, abandoned for the week as students were home for winter break. To her right, there was a large banner hanging over the street. *Annual Taste of Chocolate Festival – Next Right.* A trail of footprints led past the banner.

She followed the trail, trotting at a steady pace, aware that the ground was more slick than usual. She passed under the banner, looking up as it rippled and swayed with the increasing wind.

The trail reached an intersection and turned right. When she turned the corner, she stopped, overwhelmed by the massive crowd swarming Harvard Square. The footprints led to a nearby trash bin, and then disappeared into the flood of people.

"Crap," she muttered, slamming her fist into a light post.

She approached the bin to look at the garbage inside. The black ski mask sat on top. She picked it up to examine the hand-cut holes. He had abandoned his mask to avoid unwanted attention. If anything, at least she could now catch a glimpse of his face. She tossed the mask back in the bin and walked forward to enter the crowd.

A medley of drums shook the ground as a group performed in the middle of the square. Some played snares, striking down with impressive rhythmic speed. Others held large bass drums, sending vibrations through her entire body whenever they hit the massive instrument. When they finished their arrangement, the audience applauded.

"Thank you," one of the performers said, grabbing a microphone from the stand. "Thank you all for coming out to this great event. You've decided to brave another cold night. And guess what. We have our first snow of the season."

He glanced up and stuck his tongue out. The crowd cheered.

"Yes, it's truly a beautiful night, and there's no better way to spend it than with all of this delicious chocolate." Again, the crowd cheered. "Now, I don't want to take up too much of your time, but I do want to say that the Taste of Chocolate Festival here in Harvard Square has become one of my favorite events of the year. It's just incredible how much it's grown, and I know it wouldn't be the same without all of you. It's a cold one tonight, so grab yourself a cup of hot chocolate, bundle up, and enjoy yourselves." He attached the microphone back to the stand and the drums behind him started to play again.

Hanna pushed through the dense crowd, searching for a man with a black pullover hoodie. There were many winter coats in anticipation of the snow, but a hoodie would stand out. He would also be carrying the storage server, which was far too big to conceal.

"Would you like a dark chocolate covered cannoli?" a woman asked from a nearby stand, holding out the bite-sized pastry.

Hanna waved her off, trying to squeeze through the wall of people in front of her. "No, thank you."

"Are you sure? It has a Belgium white chocolate filling. It's quite divine."

"I'm sure. Thank you," Hanna said, finding a gap in the crowd and slipping through. On the other side was another stand. This one had what appeared to be miniature pies.

"They look good, don't they?" the man on the other side of the table said. "It's a chocolate tart with candied bacon. You wouldn't think it, but chocolate and bacon are one hell of a combo. Would you like to try?"

She waved him off as well and squeezed through another cluster of people, stumbling into an open area. It was here that she was able to gather a view at the entire square.

Numerous stands lined the sides, all with different variations of chocolate. Chocolate espresso cookies. Salted caramel chocolate fudge. Chocolate walnut mudslides. Peanut butter chocolate brownies. Chocolate ganache macarons. Triple Chocolate cheesecake.

Everywhere she turned, there was a new form of chocolate. But there was no sight of the man in the hoodie. She raced past the row of stands as the beating drums fueled her panic.

Overwhelmed by the vast number of people, she stopped running to regroup. There was no way she would find him in the crowd. There were nearly a thousand people. Maybe more. The smarter approach was to anticipate where he would go next.

Did he have a car? She did not recall seeing additional cars in the parking lot outside of the office. It was possible he parked farther away to be discreet, but it seemed unlikely. He thought he would be alone. From his perspective, there was no reason to take such a precaution.

Perhaps he would call a taxi. But the roads were closed for the festival. He would have to go a few blocks away to find a cab.

The last option was the subway. The entrance to the station was close by. Right in the middle of the square. But the reliability of a train coming in a timely manner was unlikely, and with the popularity of the festival, getting on the first train was even less likely.

So where would he go? Which option would he choose?

As she contemplated her choices, a young man behind her shrieked with pain. "What the hell? Watch where you're going, prick. That was scalding hot chocolate you just spilt on me. Christ, what's wrong with you?"

Hanna turned around to look at the man. He wore a puffy blue jacket and a bright red winter hat with a fluffy ball on top. He held an empty paper cup, and his jacket was stained with a fresh splatter of hot chocolate. The man he yelled at wore a black hoodie and held the storage server. He no longer had his ski mask, but a scarf concealed the lower half of his face.

"What do you have to say for yourself?" the man in the blue jacket asked, waiting for an apology.

The man in the hoodie was about to speak when he saw Hanna staring at him. They locked eyes, both in shock.

"Don't ignore me," the other man said. "Look at me when I'm talking to you."

The man in the hoodie turned back to the disgruntled man. He held his glare for a short moment, and then exploded into a full sprint.

The man in the jacket threw his hands in the air. "Where the hell are you going, prick?"

Hanna burst back into the chase, sprinting through the crowd, and swiping past the man covered in hot chocolate. She weaved between the lines of people waiting for their free chocolate. Raced past the vendors, who were ready to offer their samples. Slid past the performers, who were beating their drums even faster than before. She whizzed past everyone, locking her sight on the top of the black hoodie, watching it bob up and down thirty feet in front of her.

They left the square, away from the people and toward the river. A steady gust of wind swept in from the waterfront, throwing flurries of snow at her face. The thin coat on the ground was now a healthy heap. Her shoes crunched down with every step.

She watched the man approach the waterfront, expecting him to turn either left or right to run along the riverbank, but instead, he hopped the guardrail and scurried onto the frozen water. Her eyes widened, but she kept her stride. The river was at least five-hundred feet across to the other side. The man was insane. Or desperate. Or both. The question was, would she follow?

He was probably the one who had framed Eileen. That was unacceptable. She would not let Eileen go to jail for three murders she did not commit. Whoever this masked man was, she needed to catch him.

She vaulted over the guardrail and landed on the ice. Before moving forward, she shifted her weight to test its strength. It seemed thick enough, but it would weaken as she got farther out. She would have to move with caution.

Her shoes were old, and the treads were worn. On the slick surface, she could barely even stand upright. She glanced up to see the man struggling as well. He waddled along the ice, glancing over his shoulder to see if she was still there. When their eyes met, Hanna held contact and shook her head.

"I'm going to catch you, asshole! You've got nowhere to run!"

He ignored her and continued to waddle. Hanna focused back on her own feet, experimenting with sliding instead of stepping. She pushed forward and slid a comfortable distance. Then, she shifted her weight to the other foot and did the same thing. Her momentum carried over and pushed her forward even more. A grin formed on her face. This would work.

She moved across the ice with a skater-like stride, sliding from side to side and using the slick ice to her advantage. When she looked up again, she saw that the man had still not figured out how to traverse the frozen river. He took baby steps, inching forward little by little with the storage server tucked under his arm.

Hanna was closing the gap, but she was not sure what to do once she reached him. Pull off his scarf to reveal his face? Grab the server from him? Sucker punch him while his back was turned? She was approaching fast and would have to choose soon.

She hurdled toward him at an alarming speed, with no method to slow herself down. The only way to stop was to collide with the man, who had not yet noticed how close she was. She extended her arms forward to brace for impact.

As she reached for the server, the man twisted around and sidestepped out of her way. She fell forward with her entire body kicking up behind her. The momentum of her swinging arms threw her face downward, slamming her cheek into the ice.

She shut her eyes, but her vision still lit up with stars. She stayed on the ground, struck with a hazy confusion as her senses attempted to crawl back into her body. The biting cold of the ice pierced her cheek and sunk deep into her face.

Tingling turned to stinging. Stinging turned to pain. Pain turned to numbness. And any lingering pain in her face migrated to her temples, morphing into a splitting headache. When she opened her eyes, she could see the man's outline, backing away from her. Details were blurry, and colors were distorted, but she could still tell. He was escaping.

She pressed her hands against the frigid ice and lifted herself up to a kneeling stance, glancing at the spot where her face had hit. There was a red splotch surrounded by small cracks. She brought her hand to her cheek, feeling only numbness as she touched the now swollen area. When she looked at her finger, there was blood. Not a lot, but more than she expected.

The man turned his back to her and waddled away as fast as he could. As Hanna stood up to pursue him, the ice shifted below her feet. She looked down at the red splotch. The cracks were bigger, and they were growing.

She tensed her body to lock her pose, watching the cracks expand in multiple paths. Another glance up revealed the man had discovered her sliding technique and was skating away.

"No!" she yelled, reaching out and stepping forward.

Her first step punctured the ice, and her entire body fell through.

19: THE ICE

HANNA PLUNGED INTO the icy water, sinking below the surface. As she floated up, she tried to gasp for air, but the cold had stolen her breath. It was like her lungs had given up. The sudden shock threw her heart into a frenzy, pounding against the inside her chest. Her arms flailed over her head as she searched for something stable to grab.

Her hand found the edge of the ice. She grasped it tight, refusing to let go, resisting the pain of the cold on her skin. She stopped thrashing and focused on her breath, relaxing her throat and letting the air crawl back into her lungs.

At first, her breaths were short and shallow, but they grew as she maintained her composure. She tried to yell, hoping someone nearby would help, but when she opened her mouth, all that came out was a soft whimper. The extreme cold had stolen her voice.

Every muscle in her body was tense, tightening from the extreme temperature. Her hands shook. Her teeth chattered. The cold seeped through her flesh and burrowed into the core of her bones. Her toes were numb, and her fingers were turning ghost white.

Focus, she thought to herself, fighting off the lightheadedness. If there was ever a time to stay calm, it was now.

She forced a deep breath inward and tried to hoist herself out of the water. Her arms were weak, and there was nowhere to grip. She swiped at the smooth ice, making no progress and falling back into the water. A second attempt yielded similar results. She needed a handhold. Something to grab while she pulled herself up.

That's when she remembered the boxcutter in her pocket. She was reluctant to submerge her hand back underwater, but retrieving the boxcutter was the difference between life and death.

Shivering at magnitudes out of her control, she lowered her hand beneath the surface and fumbled for her pocket. With numbness overtaking her fingers, the task was almost impossible, but after multiple attempts, she managed to find her pocket.

She stuffed her hand inside and closed her grip, praying the boxcutter was still there and had not fallen out. As she raised her hand out of the water, the boxcutter slipped out of her fingers and tumbled onto the ice, sliding just out of reach.

She threw her head back in frustration, clenching her teeth and holding back tears. The boxcutter was her only chance to survive. She needed to get it back. Pressing her body against the edge of the ice, she stretched her arm as far as she could, only able to nudge the handle with the tip of her finger.

Exhausted, she backed away from the edge to rest. Her frustration was morphing into anger, but she knew that letting anger take over would likely get her killed.

Again, she pulled herself close to the edge, this time kicking her feet outward as they floated horizontally behind her. With her body at this new angle, she reached with her arm and plopped her hand on top of the knife.

Her eyes widened, and her focus grew. She pulled the metal tool toward her and held it in front of her face. With her trembling hand, she fumbled with the slider to push out the blade. When the blade was out, she could see her ghostly face in the reflection. Her skin had lost all color, and droplets of ice were frozen to her cheeks.

She turned the knife around, facing the blade downward, and slammed it into the ice. The sturdy blade punctured the surface and held firm. She kicked out her legs again until they were floating behind her, and then pulled on the boxcutter with both arms.

With half of her body out of the water, she lifted her face away from the ice by propping her elbows down. The excess water drained from her shirt, shedding the extra weight. She plucked the blade out of the ice and reached forward to plunge it back down. Again, she pulled until her feet were out of the water.

She rolled over and sprawled out on the ice, staring up at the sky as she heaved for air. She turned her head to find the man she was chasing, now only a distant figure. He had reached the other side of the river and was climbing onto land with the storage server still tucked under his arm. He had gotten away.

But she was alive. She had not drowned or frozen to death, but lying on the ice would do her no good. She needed to get somewhere warm. Her head was spinning as she sat up. She swayed back and forth, taking short, shallow breaths and closing her eyes to focus.

She slipped the boxcutter back in her pocket and tried to stand, but as she planted her feet, she heard the terrifying sound of more cracking ice. She froze in her crouched position, studying the ice around her and deciding to lower herself back down.

After what she had just endured, she was not ready to experience it again. Walking was not an option. The ice was too unstable. To avoid another incident, she would need to crawl.

She lowered onto her stomach, distributing her weight as evenly as possible. In a prone position, she extended her right arm and left leg, planting them both on the ground and pushing herself forward.

She crawled in this fashion, alternating her arms and legs and inching toward the land. Her elbows pressed into the hard, cold surface, chilling her stiff joints and spreading pain throughout her forearms.

The slow crawl stretched for an eternity, seeming to never end. Every time she glanced up, the riverbank was just as far as it had been before. And whenever she thought she couldn't possibly get colder, a chilling shiver would shoot down her back. The cold air nipped at the wound on her cheek, which had swollen to the size of an apple.

With her head hung low, and after what seemed like hours of hopeless crawling, the top of her head nudged the metal post of a guardrail.

Drained of all energy, she struggled to grab the top of the rail. Her body ached with throbbing pain as she lifted herself over the barrier and tumbled onto the road. At first, she was relieved to feel anything other than ice touch her skin.

As the smell of asphalt filled her nostrils, she suddenly grew aware of her surroundings. She was in the middle of the road. A car could hit her at any moment. In an exhausted panic, she forced herself up and hobbled across the street to the sidewalk. From the safety of the curb, she peered down the block. There were no cars. The streets were closed because of the festival.

The festival. That's where she needed to go. That's where there were people to help her. The square was only one block away, but her feet had lost all feeling. It almost felt like they had disappeared from her body, and she was hovering above the ground. It was a miracle she had even made it onto the sidewalk. Doubting her ability to walk, she considered crawling, but there was now a healthy heap of snow, and she refused to bury her arms in more ice.

She took a step, holding the wall to stabilize her wobbling legs. And then another step. And a third. She waddled down the sidewalk, leaning against the building whenever she felt like she would fall. The echo of performers hitting their drums was faint, but reassuring. All she had to do was follow the sound, and it would lead her to the festival.

She closed her eyes and let the drums guide her, stumbling into each step and sliding her hand along the wall. The noise grew from a quiet patter to a full arrangement. The change in volume was gradual, but distinct. Growing louder and louder. And then without warning, it stopped.

The last drumbeat faded away, leaving only the whistle of the wind. No drums. No voices. Nothing. Hanna opened her eyes, darting them back and forth. The crowd of festival goers had stopped what they were doing and turned to face Hanna. They all stared with looks of concern.

A nearby woman approached her. "Are you okay, hun? Did someone hit you?" She pointed at Hanna's cheek.

Hanna touched her hand to her cheek, wincing from the sting that shot through her face. She looked at her finger to see if there was blood. "The bleeding stopped," she whispered to herself, ignoring the question.

The woman moved closer. "Did you see who did this to you?"

Hanna shook her head. "No one did this to me. I fell." As she said this, the world spun around her. She wobbled from side to side and stumbled over.

The woman leapt forward to catch her, propping Hanna's arm on her shoulder, and wrapping her own arm around Hanna's back. "Careful, hun. You don't want to fall again. One cut to your face is enough." Other people gathered, both curious and concerned about the situation. The woman held her hand in front of Hanna's face. "Can you tell me how many fingers I'm holding up?"

Hanna squinted, trying to bring her blurred vision into focus. "Three?"

The woman nodded. "Good. Do you remember where you fell?"

Hanna extended her arm in the direction she believed to be the water, but she had lost all sense of orientation. For all she knew, she was pointing at the ground. "The river," she muttered, hoping her words were more coherent than her motor skills. "I fell in the river."

The woman grabbed Hanna's hand. "Christ, you're an icicle." She turned around to the other spectators. "Get the paramedics. This woman needs immediate medical attention." She turned back to Hanna. "What were you doing on the river? You should know it's not safe to walk on the ice."

Forming words grew more difficult. "He got away," she managed to drool out.

"Who are you talking about, hun? Who got away?"

The woman's voice devolved into muffled nonsense as the world faded to black. Before Hanna could answer the question, she slipped into total darkness.

20: THE TRUTH

HANNA ENTERED THE lab the next morning, her face pulsing with pain. Russell sat in his usual seat in front of the monitors. She dragged her feet across the room to join him.

He spun around and stared at her cheek. "Holy hell, what happened to you?"

"There was a bit of an incident last night."

"An incident? Half of your face is purple. What, did you decide to pick up boxing? You're supposed to keep your hands up, you know. Protect the face."

"I wasn't boxing."

"I could give you some pointers." He stood up and held up his hands, bobbing his head from side to side. "I took karate for a year when I was eight. I could kill a man with my finger if I wanted to."

"Quit it, Russell. This is serious."

He dropped his arms. "Sorry. Just trying to lighten the mood. Really, what happened to you?"

"I fell in the river."

"The river. You mean the Charles?"

She nodded.

"Holy crap! How did that happen? Are you okay?"

"I spent most of the night in the hospital, but I'll live. I took your boxcutter." She pulled it out of her pocket and placed it back on the counter. "The thing saved my life. I wouldn't have been able to pull myself out of the water without it."

"I told you, the boxcutter is an underrated tool."

Hanna turned her attention to the computer. "Have you noticed the storage server is missing? Someone stole it last night."

"Someone what?" Russell exclaimed, twisting his body around to see the empty spot. "I didn't even notice. How did this happen?"

"Calm down."

"Don't tell me to calm down. We're missing an essential part of our setup. Do you know how much that thing costs?"

"Of course I do. I helped build this lab, remember?"

"We don't have a replacement. That was the only one. All of the stuff from this investigation was on there."

"Yes, I'm aware."

"Do you know who took it?"

"I didn't see his face, but someone came into the office after everyone else left. He must have expected the building to be empty, but I was still here. I caught him sneaking around the lab. That's when he grabbed it and ran."

"And you just let him take it?"

Hanna rolled her eyes. "I didn't let him take it, Russell. I went after him. Chased him all the way down to the Charles. And then I fell in." She gestured to the wound on her face.

"Did someone say my name?" Charles joked, walking over with Claire and Howard. He glanced at her face and winced. "Jeez, what happened to you?"

"She fell in the river," Russell said.

Hanna waved him off. "I'll be fine."

Charles crossed his arms, examining the wound. "We can take a break if you need time to rest. We don't need to start right away."

She shook her head. "No. I want to keep going as soon as possible. We're close to a breakthrough. Although, we've hit somewhat of a roadblock."

"The incident with the cooling fan was unfortunate," Charles said, "but it's nothing we can't recover from."

"I'm not talking about the fan. Someone broke into the office around eight o'clock last night and stole our storage server. I tried to go after him, but he lost me."

"I see. Did we lose anything valuable?"

"Valuable?" Russell exclaimed. "Yeah, that thing has a hundred terabytes of storage. It costs a fortune."

"Was there anything valuable to the investigation? Anything from yesterday's session that could help incriminate Eileen Warner?"

Hanna shook her head. "No, sir. Nothing to incriminate her."

Howard adjusted his tie. "What were you doing in the office so late?"

"Nothing important. Just cleaning my desk."

"Can we continue without the server?" Charles asked.

"We can," Russell said. "But we can't record any of it. The internal storage on the computer isn't enough. I have a few personal hard drives at home, but these recordings take up a lot of space. Your standard hard drive isn't going to cut it."

"But Hanna and Claire can still hold sessions with Eileen," Charles suggested.

"What's the point?" Howard asked. "If we can't record it, we don't have any tangible evidence."

Charles pointed at Claire and Hanna. "We have two witnesses. If they uncover anything useful, Claire and Hanna can testify against her. Hanna is an expert in this field. She can confirm the validity of such a testimony. I admit, it's not as good as a recording, but it's the next best thing. I'll see what I can do with our budget. Maybe we can dig up some extra money to build another storage server, but in the meantime, we will proceed without one. Despite our setbacks yesterday, I hope to make good progress today." He turned to Hanna. "Do you really think she'll cooperate?"

Hanna glanced over her shoulder at Eileen, who squirmed in her chair and cursed at Lenny. "It's hard to tell. I was confident yesterday, but watching her now, I just don't know."

She noticed Claire was about to speak, probably to question why she was lying. Claire was the only other person to truly know how well their last session had gone. Together, they had earned Eileen's trust. Hanna was certain that Eileen would cooperate, but she didn't want the others to know.

Before Claire could say anything, Hanna interrupted. "Claire, could I speak with you in private?"

"Sure," Claire said, following her away from the group. "What's going on? Why did you say that? I thought our last session went very well. I think Eileen is starting to trust us."

"I agree," Hanna said, eyeing the others from a distance, "but I don't know who I can trust anymore."

"What do you mean?"

Hanna leaned closer to whisper in her ear. "Someone in your department framed Eileen."

"Someone framed her?" Claire asked, lowering her voice and shifting her eyes to look at her colleagues. "How do you know?"

"I wasn't cleaning last night. That's not why I was in the office so late. I stayed back to look at the case files."

"That was nice of Finn to stay late. He almost never does that."

Hanna flashed a guilty look.

"You didn't," Claire said, shaking her head. "You know you're not supposed to do that. You could get in a lot of trouble."

"I know, and you can lecture me about it later, but I have to tell someone what I found, and right now, you're one of the few people I trust. Do you remember that weird handwriting we found on one of the evidence bags? The funky looking *i* with the swoop at the bottom? I said it looked like a checkmark?"

"Yeah. What does that have to do with anything?"

"Only one person is supposed to write those labels, right?"

"Correct. Finn is the one who processed all of the evidence."

"But when Finn writes an *i*, it doesn't look like a checkmark. It goes down and stops as a straight line. I checked all the other labels. All of them matched Finn's normal handwriting. The only labels with the swoop were on the three bags of Eileen's hair. The only three pieces of evidence that tie Eileen to the murders. Someone planted her hair in the evidence room after everything was already processed. Someone wants us to think Eileen is guilty."

Claire folded her arms, stepping back to process the information. "Why do you trust me?"

"The person who stole the storage server was a man. I'm sure of it. It only makes sense that he's the same person who planted the evidence. He's trying to cover his tracks. Heck, he's probably the one who unplugged the cooling fans."

Claire nodded, but did not respond.

"Given you're the only woman on the team, you're the only one I can trust. I suppose Finn and Russell are clear too. But the others have access to the evidence room, correct?"

"That's right, but we have to tap our security cards, and it keeps a digital record of everyone who enters. If someone planted evidence, they would show up on those records."

"That's good," Hanna said. "How do we get those records?"

"We can't do it here, but I can look them up at SCB headquarters."

"Okay. We'll stay here and finish our session with Eileen. We don't want to raise any suspicion by ducking out early. On your way home, stop by your building and check those records. Then we'll know who to trust. But until then, not a word about this to anyone."

"Not a word," Claire repeated. "Can you show me the handwriting? I would like to see it myself."

Hanna nodded. "Come with me."

They walked across the lab, passing the others.

"Are we going to start soon?" Howard asked. "Eileen is getting antsy."

Hanna walked past him without stopping. "In a minute. First, we're going to take another look at the case files."

Howard walked with them. "I can tap my card for you. I think Finn lost his."

"I have a feeling he found it."

"Even so, I'll come anyway. I don't mind babysitting while you look at the files."

Hanna spun around to stop him from following. "No, really. It's fine. Finn can babysit us. I think Russell needs your help setting up. Isn't that right, Russell?" She shot a stern look of intention, hoping Russell would pick up on her signal.

He stared at her for a moment, and then perked up with a smile. "That's right, Howard. You know how I am with Eileen. She kind of scares the living hell out of me. I would prefer if you were the one dealing with her. Before we get started, we need to set up her chair. Same as before. You know the drill." He guided Howard to one of the chairs, away from Hanna's attention.

Hanna and Claire slipped out of the lab and continued to the conference room, where Finn sat at the head of the table. His pile of trash had grown one granola bar wrapper larger, and his security card was no longer on the floor.

As they entered the room, he stood up and clapped his hands together. "So, you're back, and as I promised, I will now let you see the case files." He winced at the sight of Hanna's cheek. "What happened to your face? Did you get in a fight? I know I called you Mike Tyson yesterday, but I didn't think you'd let it go to your head."

"It's a long story, but here's the short version. I slipped on ice."

Finn nodded. "I see. Last night's storm was a nasty one. You have to be careful in these cold temperatures. You never know when you'll hit a patch of ice. Anyway, I found my security card, and I feel like the biggest idiot. Do you know where it was?"

Hanna shrugged. "Where was it?"

"It was right under my seat. It must have popped off my belt clip." He held up a small metal device with interlocking teeth. "I used to keep my card in my wallet, but I use it so often, it's a pain to keep taking out and putting away. This is the first time my clip has failed. This little ring part snapped right off." He reached into his back pocket and pulled out his wallet. "So, until I find a more permanent solution, back into the wallet it goes." The security card was mixed in with a dozen other plastic cards.

"At least you found it," Claire said. "Take it from me, losing your card is an unpleasant experience."

"I don't envy you. What's taking them so long, anyway?"

"They say there are administrative delays, whatever that means."

"It means they're lazy. But not to worry. Finn Dooley to the rescue." He scanned his card to open the safe, handing over the files. "Here you go."

"Thank you," Hanna said, plucking the folders from his hand. She sat down at the table, and Claire sat next to her. When she opened the folder, a photo of Eileen's hair was on top. "See the handwriting?" she said to Claire, pointing at the label. "Remember?"

Claire nodded, leaning closer. "I do. Just like you said. Looks like a checkmark."

"Right. Now, look at these." She moved the top photo aside to reveal the photo of a body. The bottom corner had a label identifying Tucker Wright, the victim of the third murder.

Claire stared at the second photo, and then back at the first. "You're right. They're different. Two different people wrote these labels."

Hanna shuffled through the folder and pulled out the other two photos of hair. "These two have the swoop." She spread out the rest of the evidence. "And the rest of these? No swoop."

"Swoop and no swoop," Finn said. "What the hell are the two of you talking about?"

Hanna moved the papers over to show him. "Let me ask you something. Is this your handwriting?"

He held it up. "It's sloppy. I know. I've always had terrible penmanship. My grandfather always nagged me about that. He would make me handwrite pages from different books to practice."

"I'm not here to judge your penmanship, but you do confirm that it's yours, right?"

"Yeah, that's my handwriting. What of it?"

"What about this?" She showed him the label on the bag of hair.

He studied the label. "No. That's not mine."

Claire stood from her seat, walking over with her arms crossed. "Weren't you the only one processing evidence?"

"Yeah. Just like all our other cases, only one technician handles the evidence. I just happened to get all three cases."

Hanna tapped her finger to the photo for emphasis. "If you're the only one who processed the evidence, and that's not your handwriting, who wrote these labels?"

He shrugged. "I don't have a clue."

"You did find hair at the crime scenes, didn't you?"

"Yes, I did. All three of them. I bagged and labeled them just like everything else. I remember being surprised by the results of the DNA tests. I just assumed the hair was from the wife and girlfriend. I didn't expect all three samples to be from the same person."

"You labeled them, but these aren't your labels."

He looked at the photo again. "Nope, that's definitely not me. Maybe somebody found a mistake and decided to fix it. Spelling was never a strength of mine either. Just another thing for Grandpa to nag about."

"Thanks, Finn," Hanna said, packing the papers back into the folder. "That's all we needed."

Finn took the folder and placed it back in the safe. "Any time. That label thing's a head-scratcher, but I'm sure there's a perfectly reasonable explanation. There usually is."

"I'm sure there is too," Hanna responded. She wasn't quite sure if framing someone for murder was reasonable, but it was certainly an explanation.

Claire followed Hanna out of the room, walking back toward the lab. "What now?" she whispered. "If someone framed her, we have to tell someone."

"No," Hanna said. "Not until we know who did it. For now, we continue our work as if nothing unusual has happened. Eileen's going to bring us to her dorsolateral prefrontal cortex, and we'll see what we learn there. It's a shame we won't have a recording. We'll need to find another way to prove her innocence."

"Hanna," Arthur called from behind.

They both shut their mouths, caught off guard by a third voice interrupting their private conversation.

Hanna spun around and waved, forcing a smile. "Hey, Arthur. What's up?"

"Did you forget about our morning interview?"

Hanna slapped her palm to her forehead. "I completely forgot. I'll be right there." She turned to Claire and lowered her voice. "Head to the lab and get set up, but don't tell anyone what we've found. Not yet."

Claire nodded. "Not a word." She walked away, toward the lab.

"Okay," Hanna said, waving to Arthur again. "Let's do this interview."

They entered her office, where the camera was already set up and recording. They both took their usual seats, sitting on opposite sides of Hanna's desk.

Arthur took out his notepad and pen. "I heard about your accident last night." He pointed to her bruised cheek. "I hope you're okay."

"I'll be fine. I just want to continue with our work. The sooner we can close this case, the better."

"Are you sure it's a good idea to continue?"

Hanna tilted her head. "What do you mean?"

"With all of the setbacks we had yesterday. First with the computer overheating, and then with the storage server being stolen. It seems like we're fighting an uphill battle, and we have nothing to show for it. You seemed so confident yesterday. Why aren't things working out? What's changed?"

"Nothing has changed. I still think we can do this."

"Don't take this the wrong way, but I personally don't think the technology is reliable enough. I had my doubts on the first day, but Charles was so adamant about bringing you onto our team. Now that we've had a few sessions, I don't see the value in continuing. Of course, we would still pay you. It's in your contract. But there's no shame in giving up."

Hanna clenched her fist. There was an urge to slam it down on her desk, but she restrained herself. "We're not giving up. I'm sorry you feel that way, but it's not up to you. This technology is the heart of Core Tech Computing. I've spent most of my life developing cerebral infiltration. I would appreciate if you didn't question the value of my work."

Arthur lowered his head. "I apologize. That was out of line."

"It's okay. I'm just very passionate."

"It shows. Do you mind if I ask about the incident last night? Given you were the only one in the office, I would like to get your official statement on record."

"Yes, go ahead."

"What time did you encounter the intruder?"

"It was around eight o'clock. Everyone else had already left. I was the only one in the office and I heard someone sneaking around in the lab, so I went to investigate. At first, I thought it was Russell. I thought maybe he had forgotten something and returned to retrieve it. But when I found him, I knew something was wrong."

"It wasn't Russell," Arthur said.

"No. The man wore a ski mask, so I couldn't see his face, but it definitely wasn't Russell. Different body type."

"Do you mean he was bigger?"

"Yes. Russell's a skinny guy, and this man was not skinny at all." She examined Arthur's build, tempted to compare the intruder's body to his but decided against it. "He was a large man."

"And you're sure it was a man."

Hanna nodded. "Positive."

"What were you doing in the office so late? You can't work on the case by yourself. As I'm sure you know, you're not allowed to look at the case files alone. So, what were you doing?"

Hanna tried to recall the lie she had told Charles and Howard. "Nothing important. Just cleaning the kitchen."

"You weren't working on the case."

She shook her head.

"Okay," Arthur said. "It happened at eight o'clock, the suspect is a large male, and you were staying late to…" he glanced at his notes. "To clean the kitchen."

"That's right," Hanna said, hoping her smile didn't look forced.

"Do you have any other details that could help us identify the intruder?"

She did, but she didn't want to reveal the mysterious handwriting to Arthur. "Nope. That just about covers it. I know it's not much."

"It's plenty," he said, closing his notepad. "We'll do our best to track down your equipment, but right now, the focus should still be on the case. That is, if you still believe we should continue."

Hanna stood up and walked to the door. "I do."

Arthur remained seated, but twisted around. "I admire your passion. Good luck today."

She left the room with a feeling of uneasiness. The questions Arthur had asked felt combative. He was insistent on ending their use of thought-hopping. He had expressed a reluctance of technology in the past, but this time his motives felt different. He had also brought up the rules in her contract. It was like he already knew she had broken them and was trying to guilt her about it.

When she reached the lab, Eileen was screaming obscenities. Howard held her down in the chair as

Russell fastened the straps around her wrists and ankles "No!" she yelled. "I changed my mind. I won't let you do this anymore. I won't let you into my head. I won't let you see the truth."

Charles stood across from her with his hands in his pockets. "I'm afraid you don't have a choice. We'll sedate you, and once we're inside, we'll find what we need."

"You're liars," she said. "You'll make it up like you made everything else up. I'm going to make this as difficult as possible for you. If you want to see me in prison, you're going to struggle every inch of the way."

Hanna studied Eileen's face. They had told her to act defiant, but her behavior now seemed genuine.

"Sir," Hanna said to Charles, lowering her voice. "Could Claire and I speak with Eileen in private?"

"You're free to try, but look at her." He glanced at the snarling woman drooling with rage. "If I were a betting man, I'd say she's ready to rip out the throat of whoever speaks to her next. Whatever happened in your session yesterday must have riled her up."

"We'll be fine. But it can only be Claire and I in the room. Absolutely no one else."

Charles looked at Russell. "Are the straps secure?"

Russell tightened the last strap around her ankle and gave a thumbs up.

Charles nodded and looked at Hanna. "The two of you have five minutes." He turned to the others. "Everyone else clear the room. Claire and Hanna want to speak with Ms. Warner alone. Let's give them some privacy."

Everyone emptied out, leaving just the three of them. Hanna and Claire took a seat across from Eileen.

"Are you being serious?" Hanna asked. "Have you really changed your mind about helping us, or is this part of the act?"

Eileen avoided eye contact. "Nope. I'm not doing it anymore, and there's nothing you can say to change my mind."

"Someone framed you," Hanna said.

Eileen finally looked at her. "What did you say?"

"Claire and I have reason to believe that someone has framed you. They planted false evidence connecting you to the crime scenes. We don't know who it was, but we know you're innocent."

"Then tell everyone else. If you can clear my name, tell the others and get me out of here."

"I'm afraid it's not that simple. Someone in the SCB framed you, and we think it's someone on our team. I have my suspicions about Agent Arthur Freeman, but I have no hard evidence."

"Really?" Claire asked. "You think it's Arthur?"

"I don't know what to think, but I'm not ruling out the possibility. Until we know for sure, we need to put on a show." Hanna turned back to Eileen. "And the show they want to see right now is for you to cooperate."

Eileen scrunched her face. "I thought I was supposed to act like I wasn't cooperating. They're not supposed to know we're working together."

Hanna sighed. "I'm going to be honest with you because I think you deserve complete transparency. The SCB knew what we were doing. They knew about the act. It was their plan to pretend like they didn't. They wanted you to think we were working independently. But this time it's real. This conversation is strictly between the three of us. We need to keep it that way, and the best way to do that is to play along."

Eileen flashed a look of skepticism.

"Look," Claire said. "We both know you're innocent, but no one else does. If you let us in, your mind will reveal the truth for us. No tricks. Just me and Hanna. You can trust us."

Eileen glanced at her wrists, and then back up at Hanna. "No restraints. No sedation. Then I'll do it."

Hanna smiled. "Done."

She stood up to unstrap her wrists. Claire helped with her ankles. Once she was free, Eileen stood up and stretched her legs.

"What the hell is going on?" Charles asked, walking back into the room with the others. "Get her back in that chair, right now."

Claire rushed over to hold him back. "Please, sir. It was her request."

"I don't care about her requests. She's our prime suspect in a serial murder case. She needs to be restrained. Howard, get her back in the chair."

Howard obeyed his order and walked over, but Hanna stood in his way. "Please, just listen. We need to reach her dorsolateral prefrontal cortex, and these are her terms for letting us in. No restraints. No sedation."

Howard stopped and waited for Charles to make a decision.

After stroking his beard for a moment, Charles pointed his finger at Eileen. "Okay, but no funny business. If there's even a hint you're trying to escape, we're stopping everything and doing it my way. Do you understand?"

Eileen sneered. "Yes, your majesty."

"You will call me Agent Ward. You don't want to test my patience. You're already on thin ice. The only reason I'm even considering this is because Claire is one of my top agents."

"Sorry, Agent Ward," Eileen said, bowing her head. "Could I bother you for a glass of water? My throat is dry."

Charles sighed. "Arthur, get her some water from the kitchen."

Arthur nodded and scurried out.

"Lenny, keep an eye on the computer. Double check all the connections and make sure no one tampers with it while they're in there. We don't want yesterday to repeat itself."

Lenny took a guarded stance in front of the computer. "Will do, boss."

"And Howard, prepare the Passiflora sedative." He pointed to the milkcrate by the control panel. "Have it ready. If she gets violent, put her under."

"I'm not going to get violent," Eileen said, rolling her eyes. "I just want to be awake for this. Is that too much to ask?"

Arthur returned with a paper cup full of water. Eileen saw him and tried to grab the cup, but Howard stood in her way, digging through to find the sedative. She peeked around him to look at Arthur, who held the cup out. She reached around Howard, accidentally nudging him.

"Don't bump me," Howard said, turning away from the milkcrate to face her.

"I didn't mean to. I just want my water."

"Then you wait until I'm done. You may not be strapped to the chair anymore, but you're still in our custody. We still call the shots."

Arthur placed the cup on the counter and backed away. "I'm just going to leave it here."

She eyed the water and turned back to Howard. "Apparently, I'm not allowed to have it until this jerk says I am."

Howard puffed out his chest and looked down at her. "I'm just doing my job. Agent Ward has asked me to retrieve the sedative, so I'm retrieving the sedative. Your job is to sit there and wait."

"Then I guess you're pretty bad at your job. The sedative is sitting right there, on top."

"Are you provoking me?"

"I'm not provoking anyone. I just want my goddamn water, you prick."

She shoved him into the counter, but he managed to catch his balance. He lunged toward her, but Arthur and Lenny stepped forward to hold him back. Claire and Hanna grabbed Eileen's shoulders as she swiped at the air with her nails, trying to shred Howard's face.

"Let go of me," Howard commanded. "I'm going to sedate her."

No," Hanna pleaded. "We have an agreement. It's the only way she'll help us."

"Enough of this nonsense!" Charles yelled. "Both of you stop. We will not fight like petty children. Howard, give her the water."

Howard shook Lenny and Arthur off. "But she shoved me, sir."

"Give her the water," he repeated.

With a look of contempt, Howard grabbed the cup and handed it over. Eileen took it from him and brought it back to her seat.

"Now, if we're done messing around, I would like to get started. We've wasted enough time already. Russell, please proceed with the session."

Hanna and Claire sat down in their seats and prepared their own headbands, while Russell rushed over to assist Eileen.

"Don't worry," she said to him. "I don't bite." She gulped down her water and tossed the empty cup aside.

"Okay," Russell said. "We're all set and ready to go. Have fun in there."

21: THE STORM

HE THREE OF them appeared on the street, in the middle of Eileen's neighborhood. The same identical house repeated for as far as they could see. Thick, dark clouds were forming in the vibrant red sky. The air was unusually muggy and there was a faint ringing sound all around them.

Claire rolled up her sleeves and fanned the collar of her shirt. Droplets of sweat formed on her forehead. "Jeez, it's warm in here. What's that noise? Where is it coming from?"

Hanna didn't answer. She observed their surroundings with acute attention. "Something's wrong."

"What do you mean?" Eileen asked.

"I can't put my finger on it, but something isn't right. The weather. That noise. It shouldn't be like this."

Eileen propped her hands on her hips. "Well, you're the expert. How do we fix it?"

"I don't think we can fix it."

"Then what do we do?"

"We do what we came here to do, and then get out as quickly as possible."

Claire stared at the sky. "Those are the darkest clouds I've ever seen. It's like someone lit the sky on fire and that's all of the smoke left over."

Eileen tilted her head up to see. "Hot damn, you're right. Let's get moving so we can get the hell out of here. How do we get to my dorsolaterus thingy?"

"It's called the dorsolateral prefrontal cortex," Hanna said. "You have to stimulate that part of your brain. Focus on your most truthful thoughts. If you do it correctly, a path should reveal itself."

"Truthful thoughts, huh? Let's see." She closed her eyes to focus.

A streak of light illuminated the sky, followed by a loud crack that echoed down the street. The ground jolted, throwing them off balance and knocking Claire over. Hanna stumbled into a streetlight, grabbing the post to keep herself from falling. The entire ground rumbled beneath them with cracks forming in the road.

When the shaking stopped, they stood still, waiting to see if it would start up again. When it didn't, Hanna looked over at Claire, who was on the ground.

"Are you okay?"

"I scraped my knee," Claire said, standing up. "Other than that, I'm fine."

"And you?" Hanna asked as she turned around.

Eileen sat on the ground, hunched over with her head down and her hands squeezing her temples. She groaned with pain, rocking back and forth in the middle of the road.

"Eileen, what's wrong?" Hanna asked, running over and kneeling beside her. Her eyes were locked shut, but tears leaked out from the sides. "Are you okay? Can you hear me?"

Eileen did not respond. Her groans transformed into prolonged guttural grunts.

"What's happening?" Claire asked, stepping forward to help. "Why is she doing that?"

Hanna stood up and shook her head. "This is bad. I've only seen this once before. It was the subject that almost overdosed on the sedative."

"But that's impossible. We didn't sedate her this time. How does that make sense?"

"The last time this happened, we used Temazepam, and it's the reason we switched to Passiflora. It was quite the experience."

"If I recall, the word you used was gnarly."

There was another streak of light in the sky and another loud crack. It was like the sound of two large islands smashing together. The ground shook under their feet again, this time with a more sustained rumble. Hanna stared in the direction of the sound. "Things are certainly about to get gnarly."

The dark, smoky clouds rolled closer, bringing with them a strong gust of wind that scattered leaves into the street. The constant ringing tone grew louder. Off in the distance, houses uprooted from the ground and started to float, ascending into the sky with chunks of debris falling back down. A lightning bolt shot from the clouds and struck one of the other houses. The thunderous clap rolled through the neighborhood as the house plucked up like a daisy out of dirt, floating into the air like the houses around it.

Claire watched with awe, stepping back as the wind tossed her hair. "What in the world?"

"She's experiencing dissociation," Hanna said. "Her conscious mind is detaching from her own self-identity. Her thoughts are becoming separate entities. This place is her insular cortex. It's responsible for her own self-awareness. It's what she associates the most with as a person, and now it's crumbling apart." She watched another house float up. "This has to be Temazepam. There's no other explanation."

"She passed out," Claire said, standing over Eileen's unconscious body. "What do we do?"

"We protect her. Russell can't pull her out while she's under, and if she dies in here, she dies out there. We have to stay and make sure she's safe." She pointed to the clouds that were rolling toward them. "We have to protect her from that storm."

"We sedated her last time, and she didn't pass out. She was fine."

"This is a stronger dose. One vial of Temazepam is at least five times stronger than the dose of Passiflora we gave her, with more invasive side effects."

"How long will she be out?"

"It's hard to tell. This has only happened once before. The host was out for ten minutes or so. After that, he woke up and the other side effects went away. Eileen passed out pretty fast though. I think the Temazepam is hitting her hard. It could be ten minutes. It could be a couple of hours. Our job is to make sure she's safe until she wakes up. And remember, we're in danger too. Be ready to extract yourself." She looked at the clouds again. They were moving faster and the lightning was striking more often. Beneath the floating houses, the ground was breaking apart, sending shards of rock into the air and leaving a void of emptiness in its place. "Come on. Help me pick her up. We can't stay here."

Claire bent down and hoisted Eileen's body over her shoulder. "I've got her. You lead the way."

Hanna pointed away from the storm. "This way. Follow me."

They ran down the middle of the road, following the faded yellow lines. The sun projected a reddish glow, unaffected by the intense darkness of the incoming clouds. The light scattered through the houses as they crumbled apart, casting fragments of shadows on the cracked pavement. The ringing noise grew even louder, accompanied by claps of thunder and the grating clash of crumbling ground. The streetlights crumpled in on themselves like empty soda cans, folding one by one in a line down the road. A strong gust of wind pulled one of the branches down and tossed it into their path. Hanna hurdled over the obstacle and continued to run. When she heard Claire call for help, she stopped and spun around.

A second, larger branch had knocked Claire over and pinned her to the street. Eileen's body had tumbled in front of her. Hanna rushed over, grabbing the underside of the branch and pulling up with all of her strength. The branch lifted just enough for Claire to slip out.

"Are you okay?" Hanna asked.

"I'm fine. Let's move."

Hanna glanced at the incoming clouds. They were moving even faster now, closing the distance between them and destruction. She ran to Eileen's body and lifted her up, cradling her in front. "I'll take her this time. We'll switch off."

Claire nodded and ran ahead.

Hanna circled around the fallen branch and followed Claire's lead. She prayed for Eileen to wake up. The clouds continued to move at a pace that the two of them would not be able to outrun.

"Down there," Claire said, projecting her voice over the rest of the noise. "It's the end of the road. Another cul-de-sac." They followed the road straight ahead and into the circle of houses. "Where now?"

"Into the backyard," Hanna said, hobbling along with Eileen in her arms.

They ran past the house at the end of the cul-de-sac and into the backyard, where a ten-foot-high wooden fence was blocking their way.

Claire glanced at the top of the fence. "Do we go over?"

"I don't think we can," Hanna said, looking for handholds. "It's too tall. And there's no way to get Eileen over."

"What do we do then?"

Hanna passed Eileen back to Claire and picked up a shovel that was leaning against the side of the house. She approached the fence and struck it as hard as she could. A sharp ping rang from the vibrating metal as it glanced off the surface and deflected away. The fence remained undamaged. Not a scrape. She hoisted the shovel up again, this time swinging it over her head like a sledgehammer. Another sharp ping rang out, but again, there was no damage.

She dropped the shovel and shook her head. "It's not going to work. This is the location of her insular cortex. There's nothing else behind this fence. It's only the street and the cul-de-sac."

"So, what do we do?"

Without answering, Hanna wandered around to the front of the house, walking to the middle of the cul-de-sac and staring at the impending wave of destruction. The lightning strikes were even more frequent, with three or four shooting down at once, supercharging every house they hit and ripping them from their foundations. A whirlwind of debris whipped through the air, smashing windows, and destroying mailboxes. Behind the storm, the ground shattered into disjointed fragments, leaving nothing but empty space.

"Hanna," Claire said, following her into the street with Eileen over her shoulder. "What the hell do we do?"

Hanna turned around to face her. "We wait for it to come. We keep Eileen safe for as long as we can. We pray to God she wakes up. And if she doesn't, we extract. But not until I say so."

Claire nodded. They both knew it was a long shot, but they were out of options. They stood together in the center of the circle and watched the mayhem come.

Eight houses in the cul-de-sac surrounded them. All eight front doors opened at once, and stepping through each one was a copy of the same man. It was Eileen's father. Eight identical clones. They all shut the doors behind them and stared out at the center of the circle, watching Claire and Hanna.

"This can't be good," Claire said, swiveling her head.

"No, it can't. We were barely able to fight off one of him. There's no way we can take on eight."

"They're not doing anything. They're just looking at us. If we don't move, maybe they'll leave us alone." As she finished her sentence, all eight men bolted forward, sprinting toward them. "There goes that theory." She backed away, heading down the street.

"Not toward the storm," Hanna said. "Go that way."

Claire changed directions, pushing through the first clone. Two more lunged forward to tackle her. She tumbled over, dropping Eileen. The eight men ran over and piled on top of her. "Do we extract?" she yelled from the bottom of the pile.

"Not yet!" Hanna answered, hoping Claire could hear her through the madness. "Hold on! I'm coming!"

She charged toward the huddle of men and rammed into the side, knocking two of them over. While they were down, she stomped one in the face and kicked the other in the gut. She grabbed another by the collar and yanked him off the pile. As he stumbled back, she jabbed him in the nose.

As she reached to grab another from the pile, the first two got back up. One grabbed her arms from behind, while the other struck her in the stomach. The first blow stole her breath, and before she could recover, the second blow hit.

She swung the back of her head into the first clone's jaw. A sharp sting jolted her skull as the man's bony chin dug into her scalp. For a brief moment, his grip loosened.

As a third punch was about to land, she lifted her foot and kicked off the chest of the man in front of her. The force of the kick sent all three of them to the ground, Hanna landing on top of the man behind her. His grip released, setting her free.

She glanced at Claire, who had broken free from the pile and crawled away with one of the clones clawing her leg. Eileen's body had rolled away, with the rest of the clones moving toward her. Hanna sprung up from the ground and kicked the clawing culprit away from Claire.

"Come on," she said without stopping. "Get inside the house. I'll get Eileen." She sprinted at the two men closest to Eileen and shoved them from behind. They toppled over, skidding across the pavement. She scooped up Eileen, turned toward the nearest house, and ran for her life as all eight clones chased her.

Claire held the front door open, waving for Hanna to hurry. The moment she passed the threshold, Claire slammed the door shut and turned the lock. She pushed her back against the door as the eight identical men pounded on it from the other side.

Hanna dropped Eileen on the couch and hurried back to help with the door. She searched the room for a barricade and settled on a nearby bookshelf. They slid it in front of the door and stepped back to assess their work.

"No," Claire said. "We need something bigger." She ran to the kitchen.

"It's a deadbolt," Hanna said. "They're not getting through."

"There are eight of them," Claire yelled from the other room. "They'll just kick it open. Now come over here and help me move this refrigerator."

"If the two of us can move it, it's not going to stop eight of them."

Claire returned to the living room. "So, what do we do? Just let them in?"

The pounding stopped, leaving only the sound of the incoming storm. The lightning was now alarmingly close. Hanna kept her eyes on the door, clenching her fists with anticipation, waiting for the door to burst open.

Before she could answer Claire's question, the living room window shattered. One of the clones tried to climb through, but Hanna ran over and kicked him out. Two more grabbed her leg, trying to pull her through the window.

Claire grabbed the wooden bat leaning against the wall and ran across the room to help. She swung the bat at the two men, hitting one but missing the other. They both maintained their grip on Hanna's leg. She swung again, this time striking both and setting Hanna free. Hanna stumbled onto the floor, landing inches from a jagged shard of glass.

A dark cloud loomed over the house, bringing with it an ominous shadow. Hanna stood up and looked out the window. The storm had overcome the entire neighborhood. Every house floated in the air, rising up over their heads. The houses in the distance had shattered in the sky, now only fragments of splintered wood. And beyond the shattered houses, pure nothingness consumed all.

A clap of thunder and lightning crashed into the house, stealing Hanna's ability to hear, and leaving her with only a ringing tone.

Stunned by the sudden surge of energy that was channeling through the house, she crawled along the floor and searched for the couch to check on Eileen. The floor shifted, knocking her onto the piece of glass. The sharp edge pierced her side, staining her shirt with blood.

"The house," Claire said, leaning against the wall to keep her balance. "It's floating like the others. We're in the air." She stared at the bloodstain on Hanna's shirt. "We're extracting."

"No," Hanna said, glancing at Eileen, who was still on the couch. "She still has time to wake up."

"How much longer can we wait?"

Behind Claire, one of the men had clung onto the window frame and was climbing through. "Look out," Hanna said.

Claire spun around and charged at the man. She swung the wooden bat at his head and shoved him toward the broken window. He crashed into the windowsill and flopped over the edge.

She leaned out to watch him fall, wincing when he hit the ground. "We're up high now."

"That's good. We wouldn't have held them off much longer."

The house creaked and moaned as the entire room shook. Claire crouched, grasping the window frame. The wooden floor splintered as the living room split in half, cracking through the middle and separating into two pieces.

Hanna found herself on one side with Eileen, while Claire stood across the gap. The two halves of the fractured house drifted apart, exposing them to the open sky.

"That's not good," Claire shouted over the strong, howling wind.

Hanna glanced through the widening gap, staring at the ground below. They were higher than she had thought, and still rising.

Eileen fell off the couch, rolling toward the edge of the floor as the room tilted. Hanna lunged from where she was, wrapping one arm around Eileen's waist and grabbing the edge of the doorframe with her other.

"Damn it, Eileen. We really need you to wake up right now."

The tilting stopped, and then changed direction, twisting toward the kitchen. She let go of Eileen's body to examine the wound in her side. It was no worse than it was before. She turned to check on Claire across the gap, who was struggling to balance as her half of the house tilted forward. Hanna lifted Eileen off the floor, hoping to move her to the kitchen, away from the open gap. Before she could make it halfway, the house creaked and moaned again.

She stopped and braced her hip against the wall as the room shook. When she looked back across the gap, Claire was doing the same. Under Claire's feet, another crack was forming.

"Look out!" Hanna yelled.

Claire cupped her hand behind her ear, signaling to repeat the unheard words. Before Hanna could warn her again, the crack pulled apart, and Claire fell through.

At that moment, the same thing happened to Hanna. The floor split apart, and she fell through the gap.

The three of them plummeted toward the ground with dirt and debris falling around them. Eileen was still passed out, spinning out of control as chunks of concrete slammed into her body. Claire and Hanna weaved through the falling wreckage, watching the ground race toward them.

"Now!" Hanna yelled. "Extract now!"

Claire nodded and closed her eyes. After a moment, her body vanished.

Hanna flipped over, watching Eileen drift farther away. "I'm so sorry," she whispered. Then, with deep regret, she closed her eyes to extract, abandoning her chance to exonerate an innocent woman.

*****

Hanna's eyes shot open as she woke up in her chair. She pulled off her headband and jumped out of her seat.

"What the hell happened?" Russell asked, pointing at one of the monitors. "Eileen's brain activity just plummeted. I haven't pulled her out yet."

Hanna rushed over to Eileen's chair and placed two fingers on her pulse. There was none. "She's dead."

Russell stood from the control panel. "Dead? What did you do to her in there?"

Hanna ignored the question and searched Eileen's pockets.

With no answer from Hanna, he turned to Claire. "What did you do to her?"

Claire scooped the paper cup off the floor and brought it to her nose. "We didn't do anything. Things got crazy before we even started."

"Crazy? What kind of crazy?"

Hanna found nothing in Eileen's pants pockets and moved onto her breast pocket, where she found two empty vials. "Temazepam crazy," she said, holding them up. "The whole session was out of control because someone gave her two vials of Temazepam."

Arthur glanced at the milkcrate of sedatives. "She must have nicked them during the scuffle and slipped them into her water. We shouldn't have let her walk around like that."

Hanna gave Arthur a curious look. "You think she did this to herself? Why would she do that?"

"Because we backed her into a corner," Howard said. "She knew we were going to find out the truth, and she decided to take her own life instead of living the rest of it in prison."

Claire placed the cup on the counter and stood beside Hanna. "She fought against us all this way, and now you think she just gave up?"

"I think this was her way of fighting back. She went out on her own terms."

"It makes sense to me," Charles said. "There was already substantial evidence against her, and with all of this talk about her dorsolateral prefrontal cortex." He shook his head and shrugged. "She felt she had no other choice."

"So, what now?" Hanna asked.

"As far as I'm concerned, this case is closed. There's some cleanup to do regarding Ms. Warner's death, not to mention dealing with the press, but your work is done."

"The press will eat this up," Howard said. "And for once, we come out looking like the good guys. The team who caught the Beantown Slasher. It's about time the SCB gets a little positive coverage."

"I would have preferred to take her alive," Charles said, "but removing a killer from the street is always a good thing. Hanna, we'll finish your paperwork back at SCB headquarters. Once you sign, you'll receive your payment. The SCB thanks you for your help. Lenny, call this in. Get someone to bag her up."

The others cleared the room, but Hanna stayed behind. She stared at the dead body, lowering her head with shame, repeating her final words to Eileen. "I'm so sorry."

22: THE LIAR

HANNA ENTERED THE expansive room, following the rest of the team through rows of cubicles that ran from wall to wall.

A phone rang from one of the desks, but it was impossible to tell which one in the sea of cubes. The mechanical sounds of a copy machine rattled in the corner as a woman struggled to fix a paper jam. A water cooler bubbled as two men stood around it, talking about the football game from the night before.

Hanna imagined these were the sounds of a typical office. Having never worked at a large company herself, she could only wonder if it was as mundane as everyone had made it out to be. Observing the office in person, it was exactly what she expected.

"I appreciate you coming back with us," Charles said, leading her down the aisle of cubes toward his own office in the back. "I know it's been a long day. I didn't expect to get back so late."

"No worries," Hanna said. "I wanted to see your office anyway. It's just a shame Russell couldn't come. He would have loved to see this. It's very big."

"This isn't our area. We share the building with Greater Boston Homicide. They have a much bigger team, since they juggle more cases. The SCB has a separate area in the back. We have a good amount of space as well, but our recent lack of success has stifled our growth."

"I've heard. It's on the news all the time."

"Yeah," Howard said. "The media won't shut up about it. It's like they want us to fail."

Lenny plucked the wool hat off his head and stuffed it into his coat pocket. "It makes for a better story. People like to complain, and federal agencies are an easy target."

"This case will shut them up," Howard said. "The Beantown Slasher brought to justice."

"The praise will last a few weeks," Arthur said. "Then it's back to the next big failure. If you ask me, the press can shove it up their—"

"Hey," Charles interrupted. "I don't want to hear you slander the press. It's our job to catch the criminals, and it's their job to report if we don't. Any bad press is on us."

"Speak of the devil," Arthur said, nudging his head toward a woman standing by Charles's office. "I guess they just let themselves in without knocking, now."

"Calm down," Charles said. "The Globe wanted the story first so I scheduled an interview with her. Like you said, this case makes us look good. We should be eager to talk to them."

He turned to Hanna.

"I hate to keep you waiting. Why don't you go home and get some rest? We'll take care of the paperwork in the morning."

Hanna dismissed the idea with a flick of her wrist. "Don't worry about it. I can wait until after the interview. Claire can show me around."

Claire nodded. "That's right, sir. I'll take care of her."

"If you insist," Charles said. He pointed at Howard. "I want you in there for the interview as well. You know this case better than anyone."

Howard nodded. "Yes, sir."

The two of them split off to greet the journalist. Arthur and Lenny dispersed as well, Arthur to the kitchen, and Lenny to the restroom.

"I better get going too," Finn said. He held up the safe with the case files inside. "I need to get this back to the evidence room."

"Could I come along?" Hanna asked. "I was hoping to see the evidence room at some point."

Finn shook his head. "No can do. Only crime scene technicians are allowed in there. Not even Charles is supposed to go in. It's kind of silly, if you think about it. He has a much higher clearance level than I do. But rules are rules. They just have to fix the issue with our cards. As it is right now, it doesn't distinguish between technicians and others. Almost anyone with a card can just walk right in. It kind of defeats the purpose of having the cards at all. But hey, it's a new system, and they're still working out the kinks. You can't fault them for that."

"It's not that new anymore," Claire said.

Finn shrugged. "Maybe I'm too forgiving. The bottom line is, I can't let you into the evidence room."

Claire patted his shoulder. "That's alright. I can show her where our team sits, instead."

"She'll like that. It's not as exciting as the evidence room, but we handle all of the big cases, which means we get the fancy section of the office." He started to walk away. "If I don't see you again before you leave, have a great night." He pumped his fist and cheered as he walked down the hall. "It's over, everyone! The Beantown Slasher slashes no more!"

Claire nudged Hanna's arm. "Come on. I'll show you our section of the building."

They walked past Charles's office and down a separate hallway. Hanna glanced over her shoulder as they left the main building. "It's all the way over here? It's kind of far from everyone else, isn't it?"

"We handle high-profile cases, so privacy is a big concern. Technically, we're in a different building. They connected the two to bring us closer but, personally, I liked it better when we were separate."

"Charles's office is in the main building?"

Claire nodded. "That's right. He runs the SCB, but he also oversees many Greater Boston Homicide cases. He stops by our section every once in a while, but he usually doesn't spend much time with us unless it's a big case. Howard is really the one in charge of our group."

"So, all of you report to Howard?"

"Usually, yes. And then he reports to Charles. But with Charles taking an interest in the Eileen Warner case, Howard decided to step back and follow orders like the rest of us. Personally, I don't think he likes being in charge. Too much stress. It's a role he fell into when the Serial Crimes Bureau was established and he's been struggling to keep us afloat ever since, with all of the bad press going around."

"Really? He seems so calm."

"He's good at hiding his stress. It's probably why he got the position in the first place. You can't expect a manic leader to run a functional team. He stays calm on the outside, but I can see the gears turning in his head. He's always analyzing the situation. And I honestly do believe he's the most qualified on our team."

"What about you?"

Claire chuckled. "I'm flattered you would ask that, but I don't have nearly as much experience as Howard. Lenny and I are both young. So is Finn, and he was only brought onto our team because he happened to be the crime scene technician for all three Beantown Slasher homicides. It was a no brainer to bring him on. Arthur has a few more years of experience than Howard, but he was very vocal about not leading the team. He's content in his current position."

Hanna swiveled her head to make sure no one was around. "I still think it was him," she whispered.

"What do you mean?"

"I think Arthur is the one who framed Eileen."

"You brought up his name earlier. Why do you think it's him? Do you have any proof?"

"I don't have any hard evidence, but there was something strange about our interview this morning. His behavior was off. It's like he was probing for answers."

"That's his job. It's the whole point of the interviews. He's supposed to record your progress."

"He tried to convince me to stop my investigation. He said the technology isn't reliable enough."

"That's just how Arthur is. He's always been a late adopter of technology. If it was up to him, he would be using one of those bulky VHS cameras. He complains about the digital one all the time."

"I think he was trying to convince me to quit, and when I refused, he took matters into his own hands."

Claire shook her head. "That seems like a stretch."

"We know someone tampered with the evidence. If it wasn't him, who else?"

"Maybe we're wrong. Maybe Eileen actually is guilty, and she knew we would find out. She decided to take the easy way out and poison herself."

Hanna stepped back, surprised by Claire's sudden doubt. "Or someone slipped the Temazepam into her water when she wasn't looking. You were there during the scuffle. It was chaos. The cup was just sitting on the counter. Any one of them could have done it."

"Do you even hear how crazy you sound? This isn't some sort of government conspiracy."

"What about the handwriting? Someone planted Eileen's hair as evidence. How do you explain that?"

"Finn said he's a lousy speller. It's possible someone found a spelling error and replaced the labels."

"And the guy who stole our storage server? How do you explain that?"

"I don't know. It could have been an unrelated burglary. You said the thing was worth a couple grand."

"The lab has all sorts of expensive gadgets, and they're all much lighter than the storage server. He went for one of the heaviest things he could grab. That doesn't sound like someone trying to make a quick buck."

"Look," Claire said. Hanna could tell from her tone that she was trying to deflate the conversation. "I'm just saying it's possible we were wrong. Sure, a lot of strange things happened during this case, but that doesn't mean Eileen is innocent."

Finn appeared at the far end of the hallway, waving at them from a distance. Hanna and Claire waved back.

"We'll look at the records," Hanna whispered. "Finn said it himself. No one else is supposed to be in the evidence room, but all of your cards grant access. If someone planted evidence, they'll show up on the records."

Claire glanced at Finn, who was getting uncomfortably close for the conversation. "I'm sorry,

Hanna. I've been with you up until this point, but there isn't enough evidence." She turned to Finn and smiled. "So, the case files are safe and locked away?"

"Yes, they are," Finn said. "I have to say, the two of you walk incredibly slow."

"We're ahead of the other guys," Claire said. "Lenny must have been holding his bladder for a while."

Finn shook his head. "I ran into Lenny and Arthur. They're heading back to the lab. I guess Arthur forgot his camera."

Claire held her hand to her stomach as it growled. "I'm starving. I was going to show Hanna our section of the building, but I think I'll grab my sandwich first. It's a far walk to make twice."

"I can bring her over," Finn said. He turned to Hanna. "If that's okay with you."

Hanna smiled and shrugged. "Sure, grab your sandwich. I'll be fine with Finn."

"Okay," Claire said. "I'll be right back." She turned around and walked toward the main building.

Hanna pointed down the hall. "Lead the way, Glass Joe."

Finn tipped his head and walked. "You know, this used to be a separate building. They connected them to bring us closer—"

"Can I ask you a question?" Hanna interrupted. "Do you find the different handwriting on the evidence suspicious?"

"It's not typical procedure for more than one person to log evidence, but I'd be lying if I said it hasn't happened before. Someone probably just noticed an error and decided to fix it."

"You don't think it's strange that the only three labels that changed were on Eileen's hair?"

They turned the corner into a new section of the building. "Are you insinuating that someone planted that evidence? That someone framed Eileen Warner?"

"Is it possible?"

Finn looked down at his feet, thinking about the question. "I do recall personally collecting hair samples from the crime scenes."

"Someone could have swapped those samples and replaced them with new ones."

He thought some more. "Only crime scene technicians are allowed in the evidence room, and I'm the only one who's supposed to be handling the Beantown Slasher case, but I guess it's possible someone else slipped in. It's against SCB policy, but our security system is all out of whack. Anyone higher than security level two can get in with their card, which is pretty much everyone in the building, minus the new hires."

"But it's all tracked in a digital record, right? So, if someone planted evidence, they would show up on that record."

"Yes, that's right. Any time a security card is scanned, it goes to our records. To get into the building, to access case files, to enter the evidence room. All of it."

"Can you show me those records?"

"You really believe she's innocent, don't you?"

Hanna raised her eyebrows, waiting for an answer to her request.

Finn rolled his eyes. "Sure, I'll show you the records, but I think you're barking up the wrong tree."

They entered a large room, almost the size of a basketball court. There were no cubicles. The room was open concept with a handful of spacious hardwood desks. On the far wall was a gigantic flat screen television.

"Wow," she said, marveling at the scale of the area. "This is a lot nicer than the other building."

Finn stepped forward with his arms extended. "It sure is. It's all state-of-the-art. We chose hardwood desks to keep a nice rustic feel, but they're on hydraulics, so if you want to go a little higher or lower, all you have to do is push this button."

He demonstrated on the nearest desk, raising it up to his chest.

"And then you've probably noticed our luxurious one-forty-six-inch 8K microLED TV. The picture is so clear that it's basically an interactive window. But the highlight of our office are these computers." He placed his hand on top of one of the cases. "These beauties are top-of-the-line high performance workstations. Powerful enough to handle any task you throw at it."

He paused for a moment and decided to amend his statement. "Not including all of your thought-hopping stuff. And look." He flipped a switch on the back of the case, revealing a set of glowing red lights. "It lights up."

Hanna stared at the lights and smiled. "You and Russell really would get along." She wandered around and noticed a doorway leading to an empty room. "What's in there?"

"Nothing yet. Charles says he has plans for that room, but he won't tell us what they are. It's a big waste of space, if you ask me." He stepped toward the room. "Do you want to take a look?"

"No, that's okay. If you don't mind, I would like to skip the rest of the tour and get to those security records."

"Yeah, sure thing," Finn said, moving to his desk. "I just have to boot up my computer. Take a seat."

He slid out an extra chair from under his desk. She sat down and watched both of his monitors light up. The

SCB crest appeared on the screen with a loading bar underneath.

"So, you think it's possible Eileen was innocent," Finn said, twirling his thumbs and watching the bar fill up. "It's hard for me to believe. The few times I spoke with her, she was pretty hostile."

"She was sexist, for sure. Hated men. But I don't think she was a killer."

Finn leaned back in his seat. "She was nuts. That's what she was."

"Yeah, well, being nuts isn't a crime."

"If she wasn't responsible for the murders, who was?"

"Beats me. The girlfriend. The wife. Who knows? I'm more concerned about who framed Eileen. Being nuts isn't a crime, but forging evidence sure as hell is."

The loading bar filled up and Finn's cluttered desktop appeared. He leaned forward to search through the icons, clicking on the SCB database. "So, let me get this straight. Since I'm the only one authorized to enter the evidence room for the Beantown Slasher case, these records should only show my name. But you think someone else will be on here."

Hanna nodded, staring at the screen. "That's the theory."

"And who do you expect to find?"

At the moment, Hanna suspected Arthur, but she didn't want to reveal her suspicions to Finn. "No one in particular. But there must be someone."

"Okay," Finn said. "Here we are. The list of every person who has entered the evidence room, sorted by date and time. Of course, there are other people on here, since it includes Greater Boston Homicide cases as well. I recognize most of these names. They're all crime scene technicians, like me. But we can filter this down to just the Beantown Slasher case." He typed the case number into the bar at the top of the screen and all of the names disappeared except for Finn Dooley.

Hanna scanned through every line, her eyes racing up and down as Finn scrolled through the page. She was determined to find a second name somewhere on the list. All she saw was Finn Dooley, repeated over and over. Maybe Claire was right. Maybe her conspiracy theory was nothing more than a distraction from the truth.

And then she saw it. The name stuck out like a sore thumb. It was not Arthur Freeman, like she had expected. It was Claire Foster.

"Holy crap," Finn said as he read the name. "Claire entered the evidence room three times. Once after each crime scene was processed." He turned to Hanna. "What does this mean?"

Hanna did not respond. She slid her chair away from the desk and stared at the floor, her mind struggling to process the discovery. Claire had stood by her side from the start. She was the one who had suggested Core Tech Computing to Charles. She was the one person Hanna thought she could trust. But not anymore. Now, it was all a lie.

"What do you think of our space?" Claire asked, entering the room. "It's nice, isn't it?"

Hanna snapped out of her trance and looked up at Claire, not uttering a single word.

Claire glanced at Finn, and then back at Hanna. "Is everything okay?"

Without acknowledging the question, Hanna stood up, walked past Claire, and stormed out of the room.

"Hanna," Claire called. "Where are you going?"

Her voice faded as Hanna marched toward the main building. She had to tell Charles. She didn't know what she would say, but she knew she had to say something. When she arrived at his office, the journalist was leaving. Charles shook the woman's hand, wishing her a pleasant evening.

As he turned back into his office, Hanna called out to him. "Sir, could I speak with you for a moment? There's something important I have to tell you."

Charles smiled when he saw her. "Perfect timing. Now that you're here, we can finish your paperwork. Please, come into my office."

Howard sat in a chair in front of Charles's desk. In contrast to the sterile cubicles outside, his office had an old-fashioned feel. Dusty particles fluttered in the air as she breathed in the smoky smell of cedar. Each step she took sent a *squeal* through the floorboards.

"Have a seat," Charles said, gesturing to the empty chair next to Howard. "This won't take long. While I was speaking to the journalist, I had Howard polish up the contract. All we need now is your signature."

Howard held up the contract. "Your signature, and the signature of a witness. In this case, your witness is me." He slapped the paper down on the desk and signed his name on the line. "Technically, I'm not supposed to sign until I see you sign. That's the whole point of a witness." He flashed a smile and handed over the contract. "Don't tell anyone."

Hanna took the contract and looked at the empty line at the bottom. If she signed, the case would be over, and she would get her money. She and Russell could buy new equipment. Build a new storage server. Replace the main computer. They could invest in better headbands and streamline their software. Core Tech Computing would not only survive, it would thrive.

"May I have a pen, please?" she asked.

Howard handed his pen over. When she accepted it with her left hand, he chuckled. "That's right. You're a lefty like me. I almost forgot."

Hanna grinned, raising her left hand. "We're a rare breed." When she looked back at the piece of paper, her eyes were drawn to Howard's name. Above his signature, the line had requested his full name in print. Howard Grimley. The *i* in his last name swooped to the left at the bottom, like a checkmark.

It was then she remembered Claire had lost her security card. She could not have entered the evidence room. Someone else had taken her card, and now she knew who that person was.

Howard was the one who planted the hair samples. Howard was the one who stole the storage server. And Howard was the one who poisoned Eileen Warner.

She glanced at Howard, who sat comfortably with his legs crossed and his hands propped on his knee. She wanted to expose him and clear Eileen's name, but she knew she didn't have enough proof. Right now, the evidence pointed to Claire. Before she could accuse him of anything, she needed to find Claire's stolen card.

"I'm sorry," she said, placing the pen down. "I can't sign this."

Charles raised an eyebrow. "Is there something wrong?"

"By signing this contract, I acknowledge that the case is closed, but I don't believe that's true. I think Agent Claire Foster framed Eileen Warner."

"That's a serious accusation," Charles said, crossing his arms. "Do you have any proof to back it up?"

"Yes, I do. Finn is the only one allowed in the evidence room, but If you look at the security records, you will see that Claire entered three times. Following all three murders, she snuck in and planted evidence to incriminate Eileen."

"The hair samples," Charles said.

"Correct, sir. Finn remembers processing hair samples at the crime scenes, but I don't think it was Eileen's hair he was handling. I think he found hair from the girlfriend and wife. He bagged and processed them, and then Claire swapped them out before they were tested. I don't think Eileen was present at any of the crime scenes."

Charles paced behind his desk, peering through the window. "Yes, I see. And why do you suppose Agent Foster would do such a thing?"

"Her motive is unclear, and that's why I can't sign the contract. The case is not closed. I am aware I don't have sufficient evidence. All I have is a theory based on her being somewhere she wasn't supposed to be. I would like to enter her mind and see if I can find something more substantial. If I dig through her hippocampus, maybe I'll find a memory of her swapping the samples."

"She probably won't cooperate."

"Which is why I want one of your agents to come with me." Hanna glanced at Howard. "Agent Grimley seems like a good candidate."

Howard glared at her with suspicious eyes. "I thought my brain was incompatible with thought-hopping. Something to do with my inability to picture an apple. Fantasia?"

"It's aphantasia," Hanna said. "And it doesn't mean you're incompatible. Claire was just more compatible."

"Yes," Charles said, turning away from the window. "Searching her memories is a good idea. It may only be a theory, but I think it's worth looking into. We will take Agent Foster into custody and bring her back to your lab. Then, you and Agent Grimley will enter her mind and search for anything suspicious."

Howard uncrossed his legs and stood up. "Yes, sir."

"Has Agent Foster gone home yet?" Charles asked.

Hanna shook her head. "No, she hasn't. She's with Finn in the other building."

"Good. Howard, find Arthur and Lenny so we can arrest her."

"Arthur and Lenny are already headed back to the lab," Hanna said. "Arthur forgot his camera."

Charles sighed. "Of course he did. I guess it's just the two of us then. Let's go."

They marched out of his office and down the hall. Hanna followed, staring at Howard as she walked. She was certain he still had Claire's security card. He was hiding it somewhere. But where?

Claire sat at her desk when the three of them entered the room. Howard took out a pair of handcuffs and held them out. "Agent Claire Foster, you are under arrest for falsifying evidence in the case against Eileen Warner."

"What's going on?" Claire asked, backing away from Howard. "What do you mean I'm under arrest?"

Charles approached her from the other side. "Claire, please cooperate."

She glanced back and forth at them, and turned to look at Hanna. "Does this have to do with those security records? I swear, I don't know why my name is on there. I never entered the evidence room."

Hanna nodded to reassure her. "Do as they say, Claire. Trust me. Everything will be fine if you cooperate."

"You have the right to remain silent," Howard said, locking the cuffs around her wrists.

As he recited her rights, Hanna examined the desks, looking for the one with Howard's name. She wandered to the other side of the room, where she found his desk tucked away behind a whiteboard. Perhaps Claire's security card was stashed in one of his drawers.

"Come on," Charles called out to Hanna. "We're leaving. Are you coming?"

Hanna emerged from behind the whiteboard. "Yes, I'm coming."

"Finn, you come along too."

Finn stood and followed them out. "Man, what a crazy day."

Howard escorted Claire to his car, seating her in the back, while Charles and Finn split off to their own vehicles. Before Charles could open his door, Hanna stopped and searched her pockets. "Oh, shoot," she said, pretending to be frustrated. "I think I left my phone inside. You guys go on without me. I'll meet you there."

Charles nodded. "Very well. We'll see you back at the lab."

She spun around and headed back inside. Now that the office was empty, she was free to search for Claire's card. She had accused Claire of the crime, but she knew that finding the card would absolve her.

She raced over to Howard's desk and opened the top drawer. In it, she found a notepad and a collection of pens. One drawer down was a library of folders, labeled and organized alphabetically. She flipped through the folders, peeking inside each one, but all she found was meaningless paperwork.

She shut the drawer and tried the bottom one. There was an assortment of textbooks, most of them covering topics of forensic science. She thumbed through a few of them, hoping to find the card hidden between the pages, but she had no such luck. She closed the last drawer and scanned the top of the desk. It was spotless. The man must have cleaned it recently. All of his belongings were organized and in plain sight. No security card.

A nagging theory clawed into her mind. What if Claire had lied about losing her card? What if she still had it? Hanna walked toward Claire's desk when she realized how far-fetched the theory was. The card was the only thing pointing to Claire. Everything else pointed to Howard. His handwriting matched the labels on the bags. His body type matched that of the man who had stolen the storage server. He had been standing next to the Temazepam when the scuffle with Eileen broke out. He was the one who had instigated the fight in the first place, and the water was sitting right next to him. There was no chance Claire could have done any of it. It had to be Howard. There was no one else.

The card was not in his desk, so he must have been carrying it with him. Without the card, she would need another way to expose him. They were all headed back to the lab, ready to search Claire's mind, but Hanna had a different plan.

She knew exactly how to prove Claire's innocence. She took out her phone to call Russell. She needed to make arrangements before the others arrived.

23: THE TRAP

WHEN HANNA ARRIVED at the lab, Claire sat in Eileen's spot. Her wrists and ankles were strapped to the chair, and the headband was already on her head.

Arthur was by the computer, holding the satchel with his camera inside. Lenny stood next to him with his arms crossed, and Howard was at the counter, preparing a dose of Passiflora.

Hanna approached Claire, grabbing her attention by standing in front of her, and when no one was looking, she snuck a nod. Claire responded with a nod of her own, showing she understood. Hanna had a plan, and she was agreeing to go along with it.

"She doesn't need the sedative," Hanna said, watching Howard grab the syringe. "She's not Eileen, for Christ's sake. I hardly think the straps are necessary, either."

"She's a criminal," Howard said.

"She's cooperating, isn't she?" Hanna turned to Claire. "You understand what we're doing, and you don't intend to resist, do you?"

Claire shook her head. "I will not resist."

"See?" Hanna said, looking at Charles for approval.

Charles examined the docile expression on Claire's face. "No sedative, but the straps stay."

Howard placed the syringe down and walked over to the chair next to Hanna. "This one?"

Hanna nodded. "Have a seat, and Russell will assist you. I should let you know, the first time can be jarring. We don't usually bypass the training simulation, but this is a special circumstance. Do you think you can handle it?"

"I do," he said, staring at Claire as Russell placed the headband on his head. From his intense glare, Hanna could sense his suspicions. He was probably questioning Claire's willingness to cooperate, knowing she was innocent.

"Okay," Hanna said as Russell returned to the control panel. "Send us in."

*****

The soothing sound of Elvis's voice filled the room as he sang "Love Me Tender" from the CD player on the table. Eileen was lying on the couch with a cigarette wedged between her two fingers. She sucked in a lungful of smoke and blew it toward the ceiling. She did not bother using an ashtray. Instead, she let the end of the cigarette burn off and fall to the floor.

Claire grinned at the sight of Eileen.

"What is this?" Howard asked, spinning around to see where they were. "Why are we in Eileen Warner's apartment?"

"Relax," Hanna said. "It's perfectly normal to be disoriented for your first time."

"I'm not disoriented. I know exactly where we are. I remember that goddamn song playing in the background. This is the night we—"

The door burst open, and a squad of men stormed into the room. They were all armed with automatic rifles, equipped with helmets and armor. They charged forward and pointed their weapons at Eileen.

"Get down on the ground!" the squad leader yelled. "Do it now!"

Eileen threw up her hands as high as she could. Her eyes shot wide open, shifting back and forth between all of the guns pointed at her.

"I said get down," he yelled again. "Or we will shoot!"

She obeyed his command, lowering down with her hands still raised. Once she was on her knees, the squad moved in and pushed her onto her stomach.

The squad leader took out a pair of handcuffs and locked them around her wrists. "Don't resist."

"I'm not resisting," Eileen said. Her voice was muffled against the floor. "What the hell is going on?"

He pulled her back up to her knees. "Is there anyone else in the apartment?"

"No, goddamn it. Will you tell me what's going on?"

A copy of Howard walked through the front door, followed by Lenny and Arthur. They all wore bulletproof vests, aiming their sidearms forward. When the copy of Howard saw Eileen was restrained, he holstered his weapon.

"Eileen Warner, you are under arrest for the murder of Anthony Higgs, Cameron Shultz, and Tucker Wright. You have the right to remain silent. Anything you say can and will be used against you in a court of law. You have the right to an attorney. If you cannot afford an attorney, one will be provided for you. Do you understand these rights?"

"What are you talking about?" Eileen asked. "I didn't murder anyone."

"Answer the question, Ms. Warner. Do you understand these rights?"

"Yes, I understand."

"With these rights in mind, is there anything you would like to say?"

"Not a chance."

The copy of Howard nodded. "Very well. Get her out of here."

The squad guided Eileen out of the building, led by Arthur and Lenny.

The copy of Howard paced around the apartment, studying her home. The CD player reached the end of its song and looped back to the beginning, opening with the calm strum of a guitar. Before Elvis's voice could start, Howard pressed one of the buttons. The song stopped, and "Jailhouse Rock" played.

"That's more like it," he said. "I love The King, but that song was just too damn slow." He bobbed his head from side to side and strutted out of the room, snapping his fingers to the new tempo.

Hanna watched the scene play out, now with a new perspective. "She had no idea why she was being arrested. Now we know it's because she was innocent."

Howard glared at Hanna. "I don't understand. I thought we were looking at Claire's memories, but she wasn't there that day. She was sick. That means this must be my memory. We're inside my mind, not Claire's?"

"That's right," Hanna said, walking over to the CD player and turning off the music. "Eileen Warner was innocent. She was framed. But it wasn't Claire who framed her. It was you."

Claire turned to Hanna. "It was Howard?"

"That's right. Howard is the one who swapped the hair samples."

He let out a nervous laugh. "That's a ridiculous accusation. You can't possibly believe that."

"I do."

"But you saw it yourself. Claire's name is all over the security records."

"We both know Claire lost her security card weeks ago. She's been waiting to get a new one. It's true, someone used her card to get into the evidence room, but it wasn't her. You needed to swap the samples, but you knew your name would show up on the records. You had to use someone else's card."

"Even if you're right, and someone did take Claire's card, why do you think it was me? Our office has hundreds of people. It could have been any one of them."

Hanna grinned. "I know it was you because I found her card." She held up a plastic security card, flipping it over to show Claire's photo.

He flinched, reaching into his inner breast pocket, only to realize it was empty. "That doesn't prove anything. That just tells me you used her card, and now you're trying to pin it on me."

"Talk about ridiculous theories," Hanna said, chuckling. "The records show that the card was used before the SCB approached me for help. Are you suggesting I planted evidence for a case I didn't know existed?"

"I'm not suggesting anything. I'm just trying to figure out a reasonable explanation because I know it wasn't me."

"Prove it. Let us into your truth center. Give us access to your dorsolateral prefrontal cortex."

He paused to consider the request, his eyes shifting between Hanna and Claire. "No. I'm not going to humor your far-fetched conspiracy theories. I have nothing to prove. You think I used that card, but you have nothing to back up your theory. And now you're tapping into my brain without my permission. That's a violation of my privacy. I've had enough of this. How do I wake up?"

"I've instructed Russell not to pull you out until both Claire and I are awake."

"What if you're wrong?" Claire asked. "What if it wasn't him?"

Hanna stared at Howard, studying the expression on his face. "I'm not wrong."

Howard forced a smile. "You're making a fool of yourself, Hanna. I get it. It's your first case, and you think you've figured it out, but you're chasing something that isn't there. It happens to all of us. We get passionate about the case, and we think we can do it all on our own. But this is a team effort, and you're embarrassing yourself in front of the team." He reached out his hand. "Just hand over the card, and we'll forget this ever happened."

She pulled the card away from him. "Not a chance."

His smile faded, and his lips tensed. "You really think you've cracked the case, don't you? Okay. For the hell of it, let's just pretend your theory is correct. Let's say I planted evidence to frame Eileen Warner. Do you really think that card would prove anything to anyone? Claire lost it. That doesn't mean I ever had it. She could have dropped it in the hallway, and you just happened to find it. That's the only evidence you have, and it means nothing."

Howard was right. The security card was not enough, but there was a key piece of information she was holding back.

She hesitated, running through the consequences of revealing what she had found. It was a decision that would dictate the future of Core Tech Computing. They needed money. Without it, her research would die.

"It's not the only evidence I have," she said. "There's your handwriting."

"Handwriting?" Howard echoed. "What does my handwriting have to do with anything?"

"I was looking through the case files last night."

"Don't," Claire interrupted. "Remember your contract."

Hanna waved her off. "It's okay. None of the others can hear or see us right now. And thanks to Howard, we don't have the storage server anymore. That means there won't be a recording of this, and no one will ever hear this conversation."

"I didn't take the storage server," Howard said. His voice got louder as he grew more irritated.

"There's no point in lying. I was there that night. I was looking through the case files, and I found your handwriting on Eileen's hair samples. I know it was you."

Howard squinted at her, studying her face with great intensity. "It's not my handwriting. It can't be."

"I think you misunderstand my intentions. You were going to let Claire go to jail. We can still let that happen."

Claire turned her head. "What did you say?"

"Shut up," Hanna said. "I'm talking to Howard."

Howard furrowed his brow. "Let it happen? What do you mean?"

"It's simple, really. Core Tech Computing needs money to survive. If Claire goes to jail, we close the case, and I get paid for the amount on the contract. But I want more. Double. I'll give you this card and keep my mouth shut. Claire takes the fall, and you go home an innocent man."

Howard's eye twitched as he processed the situation. "I can't do anything about your contract. The amount is set."

"You'll find a way. Desperation tends to spark creativity. Unless you really didn't frame Eileen, in which case, you can report me to Charles and void my contract." She leaned forward and grinned. "But we both know that isn't going to happen."

He looked at his feet, clenching his fists and shaking his head. When he looked back up, there was a look of defeat. "It's a deal. Hand over the card, and I'll double your contract."

"It really was you," Claire said, staring at Howard with disbelief. "Did you kill Eileen too?"

"I did what had to be done!" Howard yelled, spraying a mist of saliva. "I did what nobody else had the guts to do. Our reputation as a department was in the gutter. I heard Charles speaking with the higher-ups. They were going to scrap our team and start from scratch. We were all on the verge of losing our jobs."

"So, you murder an innocent woman?" Claire asked.

"She was hardly innocent. She was a prostitute. A lowlife. A worthless hack who has never contributed to society. No one will miss her."

"You let Eileen take the fall and the real killer goes free?"

"Those murders weren't connected. You're young. You don't have the experience to see it. I've worked hundreds of cases like these. They all had the telltale sign of a domestic dispute gone wrong. They were crimes of passion committed in the heat of an argument. It was probably one of their loved ones who did it, not some devious serial killer. We just didn't have the evidence to prove it. They were already going to get away with it, whether we pinned it on Eileen or not."

"You didn't even try. We're detectives. We work with the evidence and figure it out."

Howard shook his head. "You don't understand. Even if we did solve those cases, they weren't big. They wouldn't have boosted our reputation. The public doesn't care about random domestic disputes. We needed a high-profile case. One that would grab the attention of every family in the state. A serial killer running loose around Boston? That's the kind of case that pulls a pig out of the mud and places it on the pedestal. And it worked. That journalist loved the story. Tomorrow morning, the papers will show that the SCB has solved the case and restored public safety."

"At the expense of Eileen's life," Claire said.

"She wasn't supposed to die. She was only supposed to go to jail, but I miscalculated in thinking her hair would get the job done. Charles insisted we needed more evidence, as if her DNA wasn't good enough. And then you had to mention Hanna Li and her research in thought-hopping. Charles has always been a sucker for new technology. When he decided to contact Hanna for help, I knew my plan was in jeopardy. I tried to slow you down, but you kept digging and digging until I had no choice. You forced my hand."

"Don't fool yourself," Claire said with disgust. "You had a choice."

"If I hadn't killed her, you would have discovered that she wasn't guilty. Our whole case would have fallen apart, and the press would have torn us to pieces. The SCB would no longer exist." He shook his head. "I don't regret a single decision I made."

"You're not going to get away with this."

"Haven't you been listening? I already have. It's a little more expensive than I thought it would be, thanks to Hanna, but no one will ever know the sacrifices I made to save this department. This is all finally over."

"That's right," Hanna said, walking over and handing him the security card. "It's all over."

Howard took the card from her, examining the photo of Claire. As he held it closer to his face, the piece of plastic vanished from his hand. He stared at the air between his fingers, and checked his breast pocket again. Confirming it was still empty, he glared at Hanna, waiting for an explanation.

Hanna smirked. "Did you get all of that, Russell?"

A voice projected from empty space. "Every single word."

Claire looked up at the ceiling, searching for the encompassing voice.

"And the others?" Hanna asked.

"They heard it too. I think we're golden, Hanna."

Howard's eyes widened. He clenched his jaw and stormed at Hanna. "What the hell is going on?" He grabbed her collar and pulled her in, coming inches from her face. "What did you do?"

She leaned in even closer, almost touching her nose to his. "I beat you."

He let her go and stumbled back, falling onto the couch in total shock.

Hanna nudged Claire and smiled. "I guess you're not going to jail after all." She pressed the play button on the CD player and "Jailhouse Rock" played. She bobbed her head to the rhythm of the song and looked up at the ceiling to speak to the omnipresent voice. "Russell, pull us out."

*****

When they woke up, Charles, Lenny, Arthur, and Finn stood behind them, watching the monitor above the control panel. The display showed an image of Eileen's apartment, with a distorted version of "Jailhouse Rock" playing through the speakers.

Russell knelt beside Claire, unfastening the last strap from her ankle. Across the room, Arthur's camera was pointed at the monitor. Russell had set it up just as she instructed.

Howard yanked his headband off and stared at the image on the screen. "I don't understand. We were inside my mind. They can't see us while we're in there."

"You're right," Hanna said. "One of the limitations of thought-hopping is that there's no live feed, but we weren't inside your mind, and that wasn't your memory. It was Eileen's. We saved her memory and fed it through the training simulation. Fortunately, that particular memory was processed and stored on the cloud before you were able to steal the storage server. I was worried it wouldn't be convincing enough. Usually, we have more time to polish the training sequences. We rushed this one, but it did the job."

"But I—" he started to say but could not find the words to form a complete thought.

"Cat got your tongue?" Russell asked patting him on the back. "Don't worry. There's no need to confess again. They heard it all the first time."

Howard turned to Charles. "You didn't actually believe me, did you? It was a joke. I wasn't serious. We both know Claire is the one who accessed the evidence room."

Hanna stood up. "Check his breast pocket."

Russell reached over Howard's shoulder and pulled a plastic card from his pocket. "What do we have here?" He held it up to read the text. "Agent Claire Foster.

Security level three. This card is to be used by the cardholder and no one else." He patted Howard on the back again. "I guess you broke the rules, buddy."

"Don't touch me," Howard said, swiping Russell's hand away. He peered at Charles. "It was the only way."

"I've heard enough," Charles said. "Lenny, arrest him."

Lenny stepped forward with his handcuffs out. "Howard Grimley, you are under arrest for falsifying evidence and first-degree murder. You have the right to remain silent. Anything you say can and will be used against you in a court of law. You have the right to an attorney. If you cannot afford an attorney, one will be provided for you. Do you understand these rights?"

"Seriously?" Howard asked. "You're cuffing me? You're reading my rights?"

"You know I have to. Now, please answer the question. Do you understand your rights?"

Howard rolled his eyes as the cuffs locked around his wrists. "Yes, I do."

Charles leaned forward. "You disappoint me, Agent Grimley. You let down this entire department."

"No," Howard said as Lenny and Arthur guided him toward the door. "I saved this department."

Charles followed them out of the lab, leaving Hanna, Claire, Russell, and Finn.

Hanna and Claire shared a smile. "I was a little worried you were throwing me under the bus," Claire said. "But I knew you had a plan."

"I couldn't have pulled it off without Russell." Hanna swiveled her head around. "You did everything perfectly."

Russell shrugged, switching off the camera. "It was your plan. I just did what you told me to do."

"So," Finn said to Hanna. "You ended up looking at the case files after I left last night?"

Hanna shrugged. "Sorry, Finn. I saw your card on the floor and couldn't resist."

"Oh. You found it on the floor. So, you didn't steal it from me?"

"No. I would never do that."

"Damn. I was kind of hoping you did. Charles has been bugging me about losing my card. This time, I thought it wasn't my fault."

Claire watched the image of Eileen's apartment on the monitor. "They have you on tape confessing about that. Now the SCB doesn't have to pay you."

Hanna sighed. "Yeah, I kind of shot myself in the foot there, didn't I?"

"You shot mine too," Russell said. "I'm just as much a part of Core Tech Computing as you are."

"He might still pay you," Finn said. "He's a generous guy. Hell, if it were up to me, I'd hand over the money. It's well-deserved."

Hanna grinned. "That's nice of you, Finn, but I doubt he will. He offered the money because he saw potential in our tech, but things went wrong at every turn. The computer overheated. We lost a whole session on the storage server. Eileen Warner died, and we never learned anything useful from exploring her mind."

"We learned she was innocent," Claire said. "You picked up on the clues pretty early."

"The tech didn't live up to the expectations. If I were him, I would be looking for a way out of the deal, and I just handed him the perfect excuse. It's the end of Core Tech Computing, but I think I'm okay with that. What's important is that we proved Eileen's innocence. It's just a shame we couldn't save her."

"We tried," Claire said. "That counts for something."

"I suppose it does."

Finn let out a lengthy yawn. "Man, I'm beat. It's been quite a day. I'm going to sleep like a baby tonight."

"Yeah, it's getting late," Claire said. She extended a hand toward Hanna. "It was an honor to work with you. I hope to do it again someday."

Hanna accepted her handshake. "The feeling is mutual."

"Ditto," Finn said. "Now, let's all go home and finally get some sleep."

Russell shut down the computer and followed Finn and Claire to the door. He glanced back to see Hanna still standing by the control panel. "Are you coming?"

"Yeah," Hanna said. "I'll head out soon. Go without me. I just need a minute."

"Okay, but don't stay too late." He waved goodbye and pushed through the door to catch up with the others.

Hanna stood alone in the lab, surrounded by her own technology. Core Tech Computing was her heart and soul for the last ten years, and now it was coming to an end.

She picked up one of the headbands and ran her fingers along the smooth outer surface. The feeling of the cold metal conjured memories of early prototypes. The design had changed so much over the years.

She walked to the computer and pressed her hand against the side of the case. The rumble of the fan died down as the system shut off. It was perhaps the last time she would hear the fans run.

The Eileen Warner case would be her final project in cerebral infiltration. The work at Core Tech Computing was dead. It was time to move on.

24: THE CONTRACT

AFTER A NIGHT of staring at the ceiling in bed, Hanna stepped back into the office of Greater Boston Homicide. The space was busier than it was before, with almost every cubicle occupied. Agents in suits were flipping through paperwork, making calls, and discussing cases.

At the back of the room, Charles's office door was open, and Charles sat at his desk. When he spotted Hanna, he stood up and waved her in. She nodded and walked through the center aisle.

"Please, take a seat," Charles said as she entered his office. "And shut the door behind you."

She closed the door and sat down, glancing at Charles, but not speaking. Her contract sat on the desk in front of him.

"Thank you for coming in so early in the morning. I know yesterday was a long day. We were all exhausted. I hope you were able to sleep."

"A little," Hanna said. "Not as much as I had hoped."

"I'm sorry to hear that. Now that the case is over, you'll have plenty of time to catch up on sleep. I want you to know that the SCB appreciates your assistance. We demanded a lot from you."

"I just wish I could have done more."

"It's true, the operation didn't go as smooth as I would have liked. Thought-hopping didn't prove as fruitful as Claire had promised. An innocent woman is dead, and now all of the news outlets are reporting on accusations of corruption within our agency."

"Yes, I saw that on the news this morning."

"I'm fairly confident Howard acted alone, but in the public's eyes, one dirty agent brings everyone else into question. Howard wanted to help the SCB, but the moron just dug us a deeper hole."

"Do you think he'll serve time?"

Charles looked down at his twiddling thumbs. "Most likely. The case against him is pretty strong. Despite all of our failings, your little trap was quite successful. It was a clever plan, fooling him into thinking he was inside his own mind, and then goading a confession out of him. You're a very resourceful young woman."

"I just did what I had to do. I couldn't let him get away with it."

"You did what you had to do," Charles repeated. "Which brings me to my next point. When you were in the simulation, you mentioned looking at the case files without supervision. Are you aware this breaches your contract?"

She nodded, eyeing the contract on the desk. "I am, sir."

"Yet, you still confessed to it, even though you knew we were watching."

"Like I said, I did what I had to do. Howard needed to believe no one else was listening. I convinced him by confessing my own guilt."

"You put the outcome of the case above your own personal needs."

"That is correct, sir."

His chair squeaked as he adjusted his posture. "That was admirable."

"Thank you, sir. I only wanted to hold up my end of the deal. I couldn't leave the case unsolved."

Charles picked up the contract and skimmed through the words. His lips moved with subtle motions as his eyes scanned the page. When he was done, he held it in front of Hanna and tore it down the middle. "I am nullifying your contract on the grounds you violated SCB policy while working on the case."

Hanna lowered her head, cringing at the sound of ripping paper. "I understand," she said. Her voice came out as nothing more than a whimper. She had expected this outcome, but it was still a shock.

She had almost fooled herself into thinking she would still get paid. But she refused to leave his office ashamed. She was proud of her actions and would leave with dignity. She stood up and stuck out her hand. "It was an honor to work with you and your team, sir. I'm glad I could help."

Charles stared at her hand, but did not shake it. "Sit down. I'm not done."

With apprehension, she lowered back into her seat and waited for him to continue.

He crumpled the two halves of paper and tossed them into the basket by his feet. "As you already know, the Serial Crimes Bureau was a federally funded experiment. The federal government wanted to form a team that specialized in tracking down serial killers. We started small, with one team here in Boston, and the plan was to expand to other cities. Howard was completely out of line with his actions, but his motivations were based in truth. The SCB has a low public approval rating.

"That's partly due to the nature of cases that involve serial killers. Someone isn't considered a serial killer until they've killed at least three people. That means the case doesn't get into our hands until three people have already died. We've also had a string of recent failures, and despite Howard's efforts to improve the SCB's reputation, his little stunt has accomplished the opposite. Our ratings have never been lower. The feds are calling this experiment a failure. That is why I'm disbanding the SCB."

"You're what?" Hanna asked, unsure if she had heard correctly.

Charles peered down at his wristwatch. "As of forty-two minutes ago, the Serial Crimes Bureau no longer exists."

"I see. That's a shame. There were good people on that team."

"There's no need to worry about them. Before we formed the SCB, they worked with Greater Boston Homicide. I have reverted all of them back to their previous positions."

"That's good to hear."

"We've ended the Serial Crimes Bureau, but I would like to start a new division of Greater Boston Homicide. That's where you come in."

"A new division? What do you mean?"

"The Eileen Warner case had many failures, but there was one big success that stood out. We discovered you. It's true, your technology didn't deliver the results we were looking for, but I attribute that mostly to dated hardware. With enough funding and proper equipment, I see real potential in cerebral infiltration as a legitimate method of investigation. That is why I would like to offer you a job. Greater Boston Homicide would acquire Core Tech Computing, and we would start a new team within our office. Of course, you would be in charge, and you would choose your own team members."

"Russell," Hanna said without pause. "He comes too."

Charles nodded. "Makes sense. He knows the technology just as well as you do."

"And Claire. She performed well during the Eileen Warner case. She's a good detective."

"Yes, she is. If she wishes to join your team, she will make a solid addition. You can choose the rest of your team later. For now, I have new paperwork for you to sign, assuming you accept my offer."

He opened a folder and slid a new contract across the desk along with a pen.

She skimmed the agreement, which outlined her role at Greater Boston Homicide. She would lead a team of detectives and train them in the field of cerebral infiltration. Her team would utilize the technology to assist in homicide cases. They would specialize in memory recall and other forms of interrogation.

"Your team will occupy the vacant SCB space," Charles said. "And we will purchase new equipment for you."

"Everything?" Hanna asked. "Not just the storage server?"

"Everything. New storage server, new chairs, new headbands, new monitors. Give us a list of whatever you need and it's yours. We want to equip you with leading technology. We're pioneering a new method of investigation and want to start off on the right foot."

"It says here I'll be a detective. I have no training or formal knowledge of homicide investigation. I've never even seen a dead body, aside from Eileen."

"You'll learn over time. I want you to understand one thing. This was always my intention, to build a team from the ground up. Investing in the equipment was the easy part. Investing in you was more of a process. When Claire recommended your research, I had no issues with your technical credibility. I needed to know if your motives were sound. After this case, I can say with confidence they are. Your willingness to sacrifice your own self-interests in order to put Howard behind bars. It was admirable. You're smart. Resourceful. You can think on your feet. All traits of a great detective."

Hanna stared at the blank line at the bottom of the page. Signing the contract meant a new start for Core Tech Computing. It meant a second chance for her and Russell. It meant an unexpected detour in her career.

Instead of focusing on people's fears, she would investigate murders. She would explore the minds of dangerous killers. She would put her life at risk. But above all, she would make a difference.

She picked up the pen and scribbled her signature.

Charles smiled, sticking out his hand. "Welcome aboard."

Hanna accepted his firm handshake. "When do I start?"

END

Hanna Li will return.

Did you leave a review?

Did you enjoy the book? Why not leave a review? As an indie author, I don't have boatloads of money to spend on advertising. That's why I rely on reviews to spread the word. If you liked this book, let others know so they can enjoy it too!

For more books by Chris Yee, visit:

www.nerdchomp.com/tothemoonpublishing

www.ingramcontent.com/pod-product-compliance
Lightning Source LLC
Chambersburg PA
CBHW051635180726

48284CB00006B/1732